A Storybook Hero

A Storybook Hero

SHANNA SWENDSON

AVALON BOOKS
THOMAS BOUREGY AND COMPANY, INC.
401 LAFAYETTE STREET
NEW YORK, NEW YORK 10003

PRINTED IN THE UNITED STATES OF AMERICA
ON ACID-FREE PAPER
BY HADDON CRAFTSMEN, SCRANTON, PENNSYLVANIA

A Storybook Hero

Chapter One

Sandy Harrison couldn't believe she was actually
here. After the weeks of arguing and pleading with her
mother, here she was, just where her mother wanted
her to be, and where she certainly *didn't* want to be:
Europe. Or the overseas passenger terminal of Rhine-
Main airport in Frankfurt, Germany, to be more pre-
cise. Not that Sandy hadn't dreamed of coming here
someday. She had, often and fervently. Just not under
these circumstances and not at this time in her life.

For one thing, her mother had booked her on a package tour, one of those, "See the sights of romantic,
storybook Germany plus Paris in ten exciting, fun-filled
days," sort of things. "You'll meet more people that
way," her mother had assured her. "You won't be so
lonely."

Glancing around the terminal at the group she had
just arrived with, Sandy decided lonely had to be better
than this. There were a pair of elderly ladies who
looked like twins, both dressed in identical floral
dresses. A couple was trying to control their three

young children who were working off the excess energy developed during the long flight. Another couple looked like a pair of maybe fourth-or-fifth honeymooners. They didn't have eyes for much but each other. Two girls who had to be recently graduated sorority sisters were taking pictures of each other next to airport signs. The group looked like the sort that only could have been brought together under those particular circumstances. They had just one thing in common: every one of them was traveling with someone else. Sandy was the only member of the group traveling alone.

"You won't be so lonely," Sandy thought to herself. "Hah! This is even worse."

At second glance, Sandy noticed there was one other person who appeared to be by himself. He was tall, blond, well-dressed in what looked like an expensive European suit, and rather handsome, despite his tired, world-weary air. He carried a clipboard and checked off names as he spoke to each person in the group. Probably the tour guide, Sandy mused.

As he worked his way through the group, his intense gaze seemed to size up the people he talked to. He spent more time with the two sorority sisters, and Sandy could tell by the girls' giggly laughter that he was flirting with them. She snorted in disdain. She knew the type. In a mobile profession that didn't encourage putting down roots or making commitments, he probably picked a woman out of every tour group to keep him entertained during the tour, then forgot her as soon as the tour was over. In the emotional state she was in she knew she wouldn't be susceptible to his charms, no matter how handsome he was.

And that was the other problem. She had wanted to see Europe when she was ready to take on the world, to find adventure and romance in Old World settings. She just didn't have the heart for it now. Even a handsome Frenchman stopping at a sidewalk cafe to hand her flowers couldn't stir her heart now, she was sure. It would take some sort of storybook hero sweeping her off her feet and away from her problems to have any kind of success with her, and they had quit making those centuries ago.

No, here she was, with a heart she knew was broken beyond all repair and the wrong attitude. She hoped her mother realized how miserable she would be and felt plenty of guilt for forcing her on this trip.

She was beginning to wonder what the penalties would be for hijacking a plane to take her home when she noticed the guide finish introducing himself to the elderly couple and then begin making his way over to her, an all-too-charming grin plastered across his handsome face. "Might as well stop this before it starts," Sandy said to herself as she reinforced the walls she had built around her heart, walls intended to keep out men like this.

Richard Hoffman was tired. He had led one too many tours, and the faces of the tour groups were beginning to blur together. It seemed like the same people every time, seeing the same sights. There were the second honeymoon couples who would shut out the rest of the world, the frazzled young parents, the elderly retirees and the recent college graduates. He hated to admit it, but he was beginning to get bored with this way of life. It was a good thing this was the last one he would have to lead himself. He was sick of the whole operation.

Then he spotted a young woman standing by herself on the far side of the gate area. In a quick glance he got an impression of big dark eyes, shoulder-length brown hair and a jumble of carry-on bags. He checked off the name of the man he was speaking with and made his way over to the woman.

On closer inspection she proved to be fairly attractive, the natural type who didn't need much makeup or hairstyling to make herself look good. She had a clean, wholesome, utterly American look he had almost forgotten in his years overseas. She was dressed in simple, practical travelling clothes that gave only hints at the figure underneath, and she looked like she would rather be anywhere but here. From the expression on her face he guessed it would take some effort on his part to make her enjoy herself. That was good. He needed a bit of a challenge to wake himself up from the doldrums he had been experiencing lately. He might have to put out some effort on this tour after all.

He forced himself to amble casually up to her, his welcoming grin firmly in place. "Ah, you must be Miss Harrison," he said, making a check on his clipboard. He tucked his pen behind the clip on the board and extended his right hand to her. With another glance at the clipboard he said, "Cassandra? I'm Richard Hoffman, your tour guide. But please call me Rick."

She ignored the hand he held out to her. "Actually, I go by Sandy," she corrected him, her voice and body language sending a strong message that she would rather be left alone.

That didn't bother him; instead it would make things a bit more interesting for him. This could be fun. He reached and took her limp hand in his, then shook it. "I'm very pleased to meet you, Sandy," he told her, his most charming smile in full force. "In fact, I was looking forward to meeting you. It's not often that I have people travelling alone in my group. That makes me not feel so left out of the group."

She glared at him and pulled her hand back to her side. With an icy smile she said, "I'm travelling alone because I want to be alone right now. I hope that doesn't disturb your plans too much."

Strike one! Rick thought, but he didn't let his well-practiced smile slip. "Well, Sandy, I hope you enjoy your visit to Europe," he told her, then turned to the rest of the group.

This was looking more interesting all the time. Now his curiosity was piqued. He wondered what would possess anybody to make a trip like this in that kind of mood. He intended to find out, and he intended to do something about that mood before it dampened the spirits of the rest of the group.

Sandy let out a deep sigh as she watched him go.

At any other time and place she might have welcomed a flirtation with a man that good-looking. It wasn't something that happened to her very often. But she wasn't in any kind of mood to be nice to any man, especially one who looked like the type to love, leave and forget. Her experience with that sort was all too painfully recent.

Still, he was good looking. She stole a glance at him as he spoke to some other tourists. That golden blond hair, with the blue eyes to match. He looked like something out of a magazine ad, too good to be true. But what intrigued her most was the twinkle in those blue eyes that cut through that carefully cultivated jaded air of his. He looked like he could be a fun person to be around, when he forgot to play the sophisticated, cosmopolitan flirt. But not now. She wasn't ready for that yet. She shifted her tote bags and followed as he led the group toward the baggage claim area.

Sandy took a position near the opening of the luggage carousel and waited for her bags to appear. The carousel gave a tremendous lurch, then began spewing suitcases. Sandy strained her eyes, scanning the parade of luggage for the flowered tapestry bags her mother had loaned her. She was soon distracted by the sense of someone standing just behind her shoulder. Without looking, she knew it was Rick Hoffman.

"Need me to look out for anything in particular?" he asked.

Sandy saw him out of the corner of her eye, but she refused to look at him. He must not have been as easily discouraged as she had hoped. She wasn't used to this kind of persistence from a man she had just cut cold. Well, that was fine with her. It wouldn't take much to convince him she wouldn't be his flirting companion for the whole trip. She forced a smile and took a step away from him. "I really don't think I'll need much help. There's no way I could miss those suitcases."

He gestured with his chin toward the conveyor belt. "Do you mean your bags are covered with large flowers?"

She grimaced. "I knew I should have bought my own luggage." She started towards the carousel, but he stepped in front of her.

"Allow me." He reached into the moving mass of luggage and retrieved the tapestry bag. "Yes, I see how you could say you couldn't miss this bag," he said with an amused glance at the suitcase he held.

She snatched it from him. "It's my mother's. I only borrowed it for the trip."

He raised an eyebrow at her, as if to say he had heard that one before. "Of course. Now if you will excuse me, I believe the other ladies could use some help. I'll be sure to look out for the rest of your luggage, now that I know what it looks like."

She mumbled a less-than-grateful thank you and turned back to gaze at the rumbling conveyor belt. She caught her small medicine and makeup kit, but even after the rest of the tour group had collected their luggage, her second suitcase was not to be found. She glanced around for Rick, but he was outside supervising the loading of the luggage into the motor coach. She made another walk around the luggage carousel, hoping she had somehow missed it, but there was no large tapestried suitcase. Fighting back the tears of frustration that threatened to well in her eyes, she muttered to herself, "I knew it. If anyone would lose their luggage, it would be me. Mother's going to kill me for losing that suitcase. Reason number 101 why I'd have been better off at home." She kicked the case that had managed to arrive, but was interrupted in her fit of anger by Rick's smooth voice.

"Sandy, are you ready to load your luggage? Everyone else is ready to go to the hotel."

"One of my suitcases isn't here yet." She tried to keep her voice light and casual. She wouldn't give him the satisfaction of seeing her feel lost and helpless.

She might as well have saved herself the effort. Rick didn't seem to need much encouragement to take any opportunity to prove just how charming he was. He immediately sprang to action as the efficient tour guide. "I'll contact the baggage personnel and the airline, then I can help you file a claim if we can't find your luggage."

"No, really," she protested, dreading the thought of giving him any excuse to pay special attention to her. "I can take care of all that. I don't want to hold up the other passengers."

He held up a hand to stifle her protest. "But I insist. Taking care of my tourists is my job. Enjoying your trip is your job." He flagged down a passing baggage attendant and told him something in fluent German, then turned back to Sandy. "They'll look for your luggage and send it on to the hotel if they find it. I hope there was nothing in there you couldn't do without for a day or two."

She shook her head. "I kind of expected this sort of thing to happen to me, so I packed a little of everything in each bag. I'll just run out of clothing halfway through the trip."

He laughed and patted her on her shoulder, causing her to involuntarily flinch at his unwelcome touch. "I wish all travellers planned so well," he told her. "Now you just have a good reason to go shopping in Paris."

She sighed and picked up the surviving luggage. "Well, onward to the hotel. I'll get my luggage when, and if, it reappears." He had to scramble to get out of her way as she lurched forward with her load of bags. She felt a surge of satisfaction that he seemed too taken aback to remember to offer to help her with the bags.

Once her luggage was safely stowed beneath the motor coach, Sandy faced the difficult task of finding a seat on the bus. The seats, like those on most buses, were paired off. She suddenly felt well-aware that she was the only member of the group travelling by herself. Most of the seats were taken, and just about everyone was already paired up. She ended up taking a seat next to the third child of the young family she had noticed in the arrival lounge. She sighed and settled into her seat to stare out the window as the bus started moving. This was supposed to make her feel romantic and heal a broken heart? The only way this trip was going to make her feel better was by making her too miserable to remember her hurt feelings.

Here she was, an hour into the trip and already she'd had to deal with an obnoxiously flirtatious tour guide who was too good-looking for his—and her—own good, she'd lost her luggage and she was stuck sitting on the bus next to a ten-year-old boy. What else could go wrong? As if in answer to her mental question, the boy next to her pulled a pocket computer game out of his flight bag and began playing. Sandy slumped against the window with a groan as the game began emitting annoying little beeps, whistles and sirens. This was going to be a long trip.

When they got to the hotel, Rick took her arm as she got off the bus. "You shouldn't have to sit with a child. I'm sorry there are no other single people on the tour. Perhaps you could sit up front with me? Then you wouldn't have to be by yourself."

"No thanks," she told him, extracting her arm from his grasp. "I love children." Besides, she wasn't a charity case to anyone, even handsome tour guides. She turned away to pick her luggage out of the pile being unloaded by the bus driver. Then, with a defiant glance at Rick and the bellboy who hovered nearby, she hefted her suitcases and made her own way to the hotel lobby. Her dramatic exit was spoiled when she realized all the rooms were reserved under the tour group and she had to get the key from Rick.

She gritted her teeth and waited for him to call her name and hand her the key. When all the keys were distributed, Rick cleared his throat and announced, "Dinner will be served at eight o'clock in the main dining room. I suggest you spend the day resting so you won't be bothered by jet lag the rest of the trip. I'll see you all this evening."

Sandy took his advice, and after hanging up the dress she would wear that evening she lay down on the bed. But then she couldn't sleep. She still couldn't believe she really had made the trip. She remembered the arguments with her mother over whether or not she should go. Sandy felt what she needed most was to be left alone for a while, to get the hurt and anger over Gregory out of her system. Her mother, on the other hand, felt she needed a change of scenery and had bought the tour for her as a surprise. Sandy really didn't have much choice but to go, for her mother insisted the ticket wasn't refundable. And, Sandy had to admit that she really wasn't getting much work done at home. A broken relationship wasn't the end of the world, but it had pretty much put a stop to her life. Maybe her mother was right. She needed to find herself again. And Europe was one place that held no painful memories for her. There was nothing here she could associate with Gregory.

She gave up on sleeping and instead curled up in a chair by the window, alternately reading and gazing out the window at the city below. By the time she

needed to start getting ready for dinner she was as
rested as if she had slept. She washed her face, put on
a bit of makeup, brushed her hair and pulled it off her
face with a barrette, then slipped into the fresh dress
and headed down to the hotel dining room.

The tourists had been assigned to tables for this first
meal. After glancing around for her name, Sandy found
she was seated at the same table with the twin sisters
and the older couple who acted like newlyweds. There
was also Rick. She took her seat at the only empty
spot at the table, next to Rick.

Because the tour was all-inclusive, there was no
menu. Instead, the waiters just brought out each course
and served it into the top dish of the stack that sat at
each place. "I've tried to order foods that are repre-
sentative of each region we visit," Rick told the group
at his table. "I hope you enjoy them and learn a little
about the cuisine of Europe on this tour."

The elderly twins, who introduced themselves as Ida
and Inez Williamson of Anniston, Alabama, tittered at
this. "We'll just have to go back and introduce some
culture into that town of ours," Inez said conspirato-
rially to her sister, and they both laughed.

Sandy figured it must be some private joke between
the two of them and concentrated on her soup. Rick
tried to start another conversation. "Is this your first
trip to Europe, Mr. and Mrs. Forester?" he asked the
older couple.

"Oh, no," the man said with a loving glance at his
wife. "We met in England during the war and I was

stationed here with the military later. We just wanted to come back and see what it all looks like now.''

''And what is it you do, dear?'' Ida Williamson asked Sandy.

''I'm my mother's business manager. She's a writer.''

''Oh, really?'' Ida cooed. ''What's her name?''

''Penelope Harrison.''

''Oh, we've read all her books,'' Inez said.

''Imagine that!'' Ida said. ''We're on a tour with Penelope Harrison's daughter. You'll have to tell your mother you met two of her biggest fans. Why, I remember how thrilled I was reading *The Vanquished Heart*. I just couldn't put it down until I finished it.''

''That was *Broken and Bleeding Heart*,'' Inez corrected her.

''I distinctly remember *The Vanquished Heart*. I'll never forget it.''

''Well, you're wrong!''

Rick chuckled as the sisters continued to argue over the books. He turned to Sandy. ''What exactly does your work entail?''

''I handle the business end of things, contracts, taxes, that sort of thing. I also help with the research and do a bit of editing.''

''Have you ever considered writing your own book? I'm sure you'll find plenty of romantic inspiration in Europe.''

''Maybe,'' Sandy muttered noncommittally as she busied herself with the main course, some sort of smoked pork chop served with a pungent sauerkraut. The others at the table continued a conversation about their favorite romantic notions while Rick and Sandy ate in silence.

Rick finished his meal quickly and excused himself from the table to circulate around the room. Sandy watched him as she ate. He definitely was smooth. He had just the right smile and just the right things to say to each person in the group. She wondered if any of it were genuine, or if he had simply practiced so long that he had elevated sincerity to an art form. It would be interesting to find out what really lay beneath his polished exterior. Not that she intended to find out, she hastily reminded herself. It just would be interesting to know, in general.

When the meal was over and the plates had been cleared, Rick addressed the whole tour group. "For those who are interested, I'll be leading a brief walking tour of the old town around our hotel after dinner. We will meet for breakfast at eight in the morning and then leave for a cruise down the Rhine river. Now, those who care to join me may, and the rest of you, I'll see you in the morning."

Sandy got up and began to head to her room, but Rick caught her arm before she could get to the elevators. "Where are you going?" he asked.

"Back to my room. I'm not interested in the tour."

He didn't release his hold on her. "You can't spend your whole visit in your hotel room. Come on, a short walk will do you good and you'll rest so much better."

With a wink he leaned closer to her and whispered, "Besides, you wouldn't want to leave me at the mercy of the twins, now would you?"

Sandy couldn't help but smile. He really was charming. She had a feeling that by the end of the tour he would have to fend off all the women in the group—except herself, of course. She let him lead her to the front of the group, where he began his spiel.

Sandy soon found herself drowning in a sea of names and dates. Rick acted as if he'd done this tour one too many times, and consequently didn't seem to hear what he was saying. Instead, he stared at her. The intensity of his scrutiny made her knees feel weak. She glanced up and met his gaze for a second, but she quickly turned away, unable to bear the feelings that brief moment of eye contact awakened. Some part of her she kept buried deep within found his attention flattering, but she still didn't like the way he had forced her into going along. As the group moved on to the next point of interest on the tour, she managed to slip away from him and work her way to the back of the group. By the time they returned to the hotel, she was safely lost in the crowd.

But she didn't manage to escape his notice completely. When they entered the lobby, he was waiting for her at the door. He blocked her way into the hotel and instead guided her back out the door, away from the rest of the group. His easy charm faded quickly.

"I don't know why you're in this mood, but I would like it if you would keep it in your room," he said softly, but sternly, his blue eyes suddenly dark in the fading summer twilight. "One person refusing to have a good time can spoil it for all the rest, and I won't have that on one of my tours. You have every right to feel bad, but you have no right to inflict it on everyone else. We're all going to be in close quarters these next ten days and it will be difficult enough without you being moody."

Sandy struggled for a reply, but she could only stare at him with her mouth open, amazed at his nerve. Finally, she was able to sputter, "As I recall, you were the one who insisted I come along on this little jaunt. I wanted to stay in my room. You really don't have to play social worker with me. I can take care of myself, and if I want to have a good time, I will. If I don't, no amount of effort from you can make me. I didn't want to come here in the first place and I certainly don't need any special attention from you."

After staring at her silently for another moment, his manner lightened and the charming twinkle came back to his eye. "I consider tourists like you a challenge," he said, his amusement evident in his voice. "I like a challenge. I don't think I've ever had a dissatisfied customer, and I don't intend to start now. Trust me, you will have a good time. I will see to that. It's my job."

He took her arm and graciously escorted her back into the hotel, all signs of his previous sternness replaced by the bland exterior of the charming tour guide. "Now have a pleasant evening and I will see you in the morning. And remember, you will have a good time.''

Sandy didn't know what to say. She just let him lead her to her room, where she promptly shut the door on him and went to sit on the bed. She caught a glance of herself in the mirror on the wall across the room. A sullen-looking young woman stared back at her, her sandy brown hair pulled straight back from her face and her minimal makeup doing nothing to enhance her appearance. Definitely not a Cassandra, her mother's idea of a romantic heroine, she decided, and certainly not anything worth a handsome tour guide's effort. She didn't want to spoil anyone else's good time, but she didn't want Rick fussing over her. She just wanted to be left alone to heal from her inner pain.

She had had enough of her life being manipulated by a man with Gregory. She didn't need it again, even if it would only be for ten days. Maybe if she kept quiet he would leave her alone. She angrily pulled the barrette from her hair and went to wash her face. If Rick thought he would get her to be the life of the group, he was mistaken. She just wasn't that type. She never had been.

But she had an inkling of a feeling there was a lot more to him than appeared on the surface. Just for a second, when he had been berating her for her attitude, she had seen a hint of fire beneath his smooth exterior. He wasn't as complacent as he tried to act. She wondered what else lay beneath that surface, and if she would see those guessed-at depths.

Chapter Two

Rick went to his room with a sense of satisfaction. This tour was going to prove much more interesting than he had thought. He was even beginning to enjoy himself. For one thing, this was a nicely mixed group, with only one pair of elderly sisters. He could handle that with ease and without hurting their feelings. That was much better than last month's group, which must have been the annual convention of the Ancient Spinsters of America. Ten days spent with twenty old women who thought he was either "cute as a bug," a perfect match for their nieces or someone in need of an older, more experienced woman was something he hoped never to have to face again.

There were also fewer young children, just enough to make the trip fun but not enough to drive everyone mad. The only potential problem was the surly pre-teen with the computer game. He could see himself having to hide the Nintendo wizard's batteries by the end of the trip if his playing endurance on the drive from the airport was any indication of his future behavior. The rest of the group were what he liked to call low-maintenance tourists, young and old couples who kept to themselves and left him alone unless they had questions.

Then there was Sandy Harrison. Although he had to admit to a bit of disappointment at finding the real Sandy to be nothing like the hoped-for exotic Cassandra, she would make life interesting for the next ten days. She looked like she needed cheering up and a new lease on life.

But was it his place to step in and interfere in her life like that? He did have the responsibility to the rest of the group to keep everyone happy and pleasant to be around. And he often saw himself as a sort of international bartender, able to listen to and solve his clients' problems. Why should this be different? Just because she was an attractive young woman didn't mean he had to ignore her. He didn't have to get emotionally involved—that was something he always avoided. It would just be his good deed of the month to cheer her up.

That would take getting past that shield she seemed to have put around herself. He wondered what the best approach would be. Should he just flirt and wear down her resistance or show compassion and care? He remembered the sad, hurt look in those soft brown eyes and decided she probably had had more compassion than she could take, both from others and herself. No, what she needed was a self-esteem boost from some good old-fashioned flirting. That settled in his mind, he got ready for bed and went to sleep, already anticipating the day ahead.

The next morning, Sandy woke up feeling rejuvenated, most traces of jet lag and last night's bad mood behind her. As she got out of bed, she was almost looking forward to the day ahead. Since she was here anyway, she figured she might as well try to enjoy herself. After a quick shower she put on a neat, practical travelling outfit of beige slacks, a white blouse and comfortable walking shoes, then she put her hair in a ponytail and added a touch of makeup to her freshly scrubbed face. Grabbing her purse and the key to her room, she went to breakfast.

The spring quickly left her step when she saw the other person waiting for the elevator. Not first thing in the morning, she mentally wailed. That was more than she could deal with. Rick looked disgustingly cheerful for this early in the morning, but she figured looking cheerful was just part of his job. Instead of the suit he had worn yesterday he was dressed more casually, in slacks and a polo shirt, with a windbreaker in a shade of blue that perfectly matched his eyes. He looked more than ever like something out of a magazine ad or a clothing catalogue.

Rick gave her his well-practiced smile and a ''Good morning,'' but didn't say anything else. He was back to being the smooth guide, all traces of the depth he had shown last night hidden. Sandy was relieved that he didn't refer to the evening before. Maybe if she kept up a cheerful attitude he would leave her alone.

The elevator arrived and the silence became uncomfortable as the two of them were confined together in the small space. Finally, he spoke again. "Did you sleep well last night?"

"Yes, very well, thank you." The silence fell again. Sandy was acutely aware of his presence just a few feet away from her. Until the elevator reached the main floor, Sandy turned her attention toward the numbers over the door. She couldn't get off the elevator fast enough once it came to a stop. With the feeling that Rick was right behind her, she hurried into the dining room, looking for a spot at a table where he couldn't join her.

Unfortunately, the dining room was almost empty. The only members of the tour party present were the Williamson sisters. Sandy took a seat at their table, and Rick took the other empty seat at the table, next to Sandy. Sandy shifted slightly in her chair to face the sisters and avoid looking at him.

Ida was struggling to cut into a hard roll. Her frantic sawing with her knife only resulted in a shower of crumbs. Her sister was busy coaching her on technique, but hadn't tried to butter her own roll. Rick laughed softly as he took a roll from the bread basket in the center of the table. "Ah, yes, the national breakfast of Germany." He expertly plunged his knife into the bread, then used his thumbs to tear it in two pieces.

"See, Ida, I told you that's how you do it," Inez

told her sister. "I don't see why you had so much trouble."

"It's an acquired skill," Rick put in before the sisterly argument could get started in earnest. "You'll pick it up with time."

Sandy didn't even want to try fighting with the roll. She didn't want to give him any reason to help her or to laugh at her. Instead she just sipped her coffee and muttered something about rarely eating breakfast.

"What are we doing today, Mr. Hoffman?" chirped Ida once she had finally succeeded in buttering her own roll.

He took a sip of coffee. "As soon as I can get everyone in the bus we're going to go up to this little town called Rudesheim, where we'll catch the boat for a cruise down the Rhine river."

Inez elbowed her sister. "You would have known that if you'd looked at the itinerary."

This time Rick didn't try to stop the argument. He finished his coffee and his roll, then excused himself to go have the front desk call each of the rooms assigned to the tour group. "The first day in the new time zone is always tough to get used to," he explained. "We'll never get going if we don't wake some people up. The bus will start loading in an hour."

Not wanting to be left alone with the argumentative twins, Sandy also excused herself. After exchanging some American money for German marks at the concierge desk, she took advantage of the spare hour to visit a bakery she had noticed on the tour the evening before and buy something more palatable for breakfast. The roll she chose was decadently sweet, but she reasoned it would do no good to faint with hunger on the trip. She didn't want to give Rick any excuse to try to revive her.

She was surprised to find that he had managed to round up all the guests by the time she returned to the hotel, collected her belongings and arrived back in the lobby. Before long, Rick had the luggage and the passengers loaded, and they were on their way out of the city. Sandy took her previous seat between the little boy and the window. The bus hadn't even started moving before the kid began to play his computer game. Its beeps and whistles punctuated the entire drive, adding to the cacophony of emotions battling beneath the carefully guarded surface of Sandy's soul.

It was late morning when they reached the dock at Rudesheim. The boy sitting next to Sandy stopped playing his game to gaze in wonder at the big excursion boat that was waiting at the dock. "Mom, is that the boat we're going to ride on?" he demanded.

"I don't know, Justin," his mother replied mildly. Sandy wondered how a mother with a child like that could remain so calm. Sandy figured she was either burned out or tranquilized. As she thought this, a smile involuntarily crossed her lips, and she looked up to find Rick standing in the aisle, staring at her down the length of the bus. He gave her that all-too-charming grin and raised the microphone he held in his hand to his mouth.

"Ladies and gentlemen, we are now in the town of Rudesheim on the Rhine river. Rudesheim lies on the Rheingau, the Rhine gorge known for its vineyards and its castles. From here we will be taking a cruise along the Rhine downstream to Koblenz, where our bus will meet us. As you get off the bus I will hand you your ticket to board the ship. There is a restaurant and a snack counter on the ship, and lunch is on your own. Enjoy your afternoon, and if you need me for any reason, feel free to have me paged. The porters on the ship speak excellent English." He turned off the microphone, opened the bus door, and got off the bus, stopping just below the bottom step to help the tourists disembark.

The tourists began to pour off the bus. Justin's mother lost track of her son quickly when the boy rushed to be one of the first off, and Sandy had to smile again when the woman calmly told her husband to go find the child.

Sandy was still smiling when she finally made her own way down the steps of the bus. She tried to take her boat ticket from Rick, but he held on to it tightly. "So, I see you can smile and mean it," he said as he raised one eyebrow at her in amusement. "It looks good on you. What were you thinking about?"

"I'm just glad I'm not that little monster's mother," she told him.

"I thought you said you liked children."

"I do. I just have a problem with monsters who are addicted to annoying pocket computer games and whose mothers can't and won't control them."

"If you like, you can sit with me. The offer is always open."

That was the last thing she needed. At least she wouldn't have to fight off an unsettling reaction to a freckle-faced ten-year-old who had eyes only for his game. "Oh, I don't know," she said blithely. "I'm trying to work on my martyrdom medal in patience. I told you last night I didn't want to have a good time. Now can I have my ticket? I don't want to miss the boat."

"But then we could have this whole big bus to ourselves. I'm so glad you just gave me that idea." He put both her ticket and his in his windbreaker pocket, then folded his arms casually across his chest, looked down to glance at his watch, and patiently tapped his foot as his mouth twisted in a wry half grin.

She glanced up and down the dock, then said, "Do they rent rowboats around here? I'll even take a chance on a leaky one. You did say it was downstream from here." With her head held defiantly high she turned and walked toward the river.

"Okay, you win this one!" he shouted after her. She turned back to face him and he reluctantly relinquished the ticket. As he handed it to her, he said, "Remember, you can have me paged if you need me."

"I'll keep that in mind," she tossed over her shoulder as she made her way up the gangplank. Then an uncomfortable thought crossed her mind. She had been flirting almost as much as he had—and she had enjoyed it. That was certainly out of character for her. "It's not going to happen again," she told herself softly. She found a seat near the rail on the top deck of the boat and stared out across the water at the town that lay nestled in the hollow of the hills across the river. She was puzzling over a small, yellow-painted tower that stood on an island in the river when she sensed someone sitting down next to her.

"It's called Mouse Tower," Rick's voice told her. She refused to acknowledge his presence, but he continued speaking. "It was once a toll gate controlled by a wicked bishop. Legend has it that when some peasants protested his policies, he tricked them into going into a barn and then he set it on fire." His voice dropped in tone as he gave his words a menacing, dramatic impact. "Millions of mice ran from the barn and chased him away. He tried to escape by taking a boat to the tower, but the mice followed him and ate him."

Sandy shuddered and couldn't help turning to look at him in horror. "You can't be serious."

He shrugged casually, all traces of his previous drama gone. "That's the way the legend goes. I didn't make it up. If you don't believe me, listen to the loudspeakers." He sat down in the chair next to her and rested his elbows on the rail.

Straining her ears, Sandy could just make out the tinny sound of someone speaking in German coming from a speaker on the deck house. "How do I know that's what they're saying? I don't speak German."

"Just wait for the English translation. By then we'll be halfway down the river, though." He gave her another one of those charming grins. "If you like, I can tell you what I know about some of the castles and towns, and what I don't know I can translate for you. That way you won't have to wait to hear the English translation from that speaker."

She wanted to refuse him, but she was interested in the stories. She might even get some background ideas her mother could use in a book. As she grappled with conflicting feelings she heard the loudspeaker finally telling the English version of the mouse story, and she had to admit that Rick had done a better job. "Alright, you are the tour guide and I may as well take full advantage of your expertise," she told him.

He leaned back in his deck chair. "You know, you may even force me to actually look at these castles for a change. After a while, they all begin to blur."

"Don't put yourself out on my account."

"No problem. It's good for me to refresh myself every so often. When I start getting bored with my own tours it could hurt my business. And I would appreciate any storytelling critiques from an expert."

"Well, how's this for a start? What's that statue up there? It looks like a lady holding a sword."

"It is. It's the Watch on the Rhine. Bismark had it put there as a symbol of German unity."

"Ah, very good. You haven't forgotten everything."

"Of course not," he said earnestly. He eased his chair closer to hers. "I suppose you want to hear the entire history of every crumbling ruin along the way?"

She gave him an innocent smile. "I might. But only if you know all that."

He groaned. "You are a stern taskmaster, woman. That'll teach me to offer my knowledge and expertise to any pretty face."

She blushed and glanced away from him at the unexpected compliment. She realized just how boldly she had been flirting with him. She wasn't used to behaving that way toward men, and she didn't know how to react when he responded in kind. She instantly stiffened.

He didn't seem to notice the change in her demeanor and continued his casual discussion of points of interest they passed along the way. She half listened to him as she tried to sort out her reactions to him. She had thought she would be immune to the attractions of men for some time to come. The breakup with Gregory should have cured her of those inclinations, yet here she was warming to the first eligible man she met. "How can you be so weak?" she thought to herself. She was jarred out of her reverie by a gentle nudge on her shoulder.

"Are you listening to me? Or did I just waste some of my best stuff on thin air?" Abruptly his expression changed and his smile faded when he looked at her face. "What's wrong? Was it something I said?" he asked, his voice full of earnest concern.

She swallowed the lump in her throat and forced a smile. "No, it's all right. I was just squinting to see something on the opposite shore."

His smile returned, and his indignant expression was so comical Sandy had to laugh in spite of herself. "I can't believe you found some trifle on the shore more interesting than my years of knowledge gained as a tour guide," he said huffily.

"Relax, your reputation is safe with me," she told him. "I won't tell anyone that your spiel failed to enthrall me completely. Anyway, I'm easily distracted. Something you said reminded me of something else, and next thing I know I'm off in my own little world."

"What was it I said?" he started to ask, but she jumped up and pointed downstream.

"What's that? Is that a castle in the middle of the river?"

He stood and gazed in the direction her finger pointed. "It's more like a toll station. That's where the robber barons used to stop ships to collect tolls."

She stared at the building in wonder as they drew nearer. "Now that's what a castle should look like," she breathed.

"I told you, it's not a castle. It's a toll station."

"Well, it looks more like a real castle than those crumbling heaps of rock up on the hills." Her voice grew dreamy as she sailed off to her own fantasy world. "I can just imagine the evil robber barons who lived there. They probably kidnapped some beautiful maiden and held her prisoner out on that island, until a brave prince came to rescue her."

He laughed. "You're quite the romantic."

She shot him a withering glance. "It's just a vivid imagination." She blushed sheepishly, then added, "And I've read a few fairy tales in my time. I sort of wish we were going to see the land of the Brothers Grimm on this trip."

"Well, then, you'll just have to come back for my special fairy-tale package tour."

"You have one of those?"

"Now I do. It's an exclusive created just for you. Would you like to sign up?"

"Hmm, I'll have to think about it. I'll wait and see how well I like this tour before I decide to take another."

"Oh, so you're one of those smart shoppers. Well, I can guarantee one hundred percent satisfaction on any of my tours."

"Really? So have you ever given anyone their money back if they didn't have a good time?"

"Never. I've never had a dissatisfied customer. Everyone has fun on my tours, even the tough cases."

"Are you implying that I'm a tough case?"

"You're not as tough as I thought you'd be. Last night I told you I like I challenge, but I don't think you're going to be much of a challenge after all."

"I'm not?"

"No. It only took me a couple of hours and some

good stories about the Rhine to loosen you up a bit.''
He gave her a long, measuring look. ''Yes, I think
you're more like that rock over there.'' He pointed to
a large promontory that stuck into the river.

''That rock?''

''It's the Lorelei. When the wind comes down the
gorge it whistles upon the rock. Sailors used to think
it was mermaids calling to them and followed the
sound, only to crash against the rock.''

''And you think I'm like that?''

''I think you could easily entice a man into danger,
into getting into something he's not prepared for.''

She put her hands on her hips and stared at him for
a second. ''Do you flirt so shamelessly with all the
women on your tours?'' she asked.

He smirked. ''Only the pretty, young single ones.
Or rich old ladies who look like big tippers.''

She snorted. ''Well, I suppose in your line of work
it helps to be smooth.''

''Always. But I hope that doesn't mean we can't be
friends.''

''Friends, huh? I bet you say that to all the women
you try to sweep off their feet.''

''As I've said, only the single, young pretty ones.''

There it was again, that word ''pretty.'' To be honest
with herself, she had been fishing for him to repeat the
compliment. It wasn't something she had heard very
often, and it felt good to hear it from this handsome
almost stranger, even if she knew he wasn't entirely
sincere. Still looking for a clarification of his opinion

of her she asked, ''What about the two college girls? They're young, single and pretty, and it looks like they have money in the family.''

He shook his head. ''They aren't my type. Besides, I'm not sure how pretty they'd be if you took away the hairspray and makeup. On the other hand, I know exactly what you look like without hairspray and makeup.''

She self-consciously patted at her hair, which surely must have been wind-blown after an hour or so on the deck of the boat. She also knew that what little makeup she had put on that morning must have been long gone. Suddenly she wanted nothing more than to see herself in a mirror so she could see how he saw her. Then she berated herself for caring. It didn't matter much one way or the other what he thought of her.

''I'm sorry I don't meet up with your standards of personal grooming,'' she said.

''I didn't say that. Don't be so defensive. You really are prickly, aren't you?'' He gave another one of those charming grins. ''Just relax, why don't you? Now what do you say, can we be friends just for this ten days?''

''Look, I really don't need your charity. I came on this trip because I needed to get away and have some time to myself.''

He looked stung. ''I wasn't implying that you needed my charity. I thought I needed yours. You wouldn't leave me alone to face those old twins, would you?'' His easy charm faded, replaced by that intensity she had seen the night before. His blue eyes grew dark and stormy, and she became well aware that he really meant every word he was saying. "This is a lonely line of work, believe it or not, and I would have enjoyed having someone to talk to." He shoved his hands deep into the pockets of his jacket, glanced at the deck beneath his feet, then looked back up at her and continued, his voice strangely hoarse. "But I must respect your wishes. If you need to be alone I should give you that chance." He started to walk away, then turned back to her and added, "I really ought to go check on the rest of the group. I don't want them to think I'm neglecting them."

Sandy watched him go, a part of her wanting to call out to him and apologize, but another part of her too terrified to take that step. She couldn't handle any kind of involvement just yet, and she knew she could easily get drawn in too deeply for her own good by the handsome, witty tour guide. She reminded herself that after ten days she would never see him again, so it wasn't worth getting hurt over. He could find his amusement somewhere else. Resolutely, she reinforced the chinks he had knocked in the walls around her heart and turned back to the rail to gaze at the river rushing beneath her. She glanced up and saw another castle on the cliffs above her, and she wondered what kind of story Rick would have to tell about that.

Rick mentally kicked himself for pushing too hard too fast. He had been so encouraged at how she had responded to him that he had gotten carried away. She had been hurt before, that much was obvious, and she really did seem sincere about wanting to be alone, so maybe he should back off a bit. But he couldn't help thinking of the way her face lit up when she smiled, or the way she looked when she was lost in wonder. Yes, he thought, once you sift your way through the bitterness she can be interesting. Normally he made it a policy not to get emotionally involved with any of his tourists. Involvement only made for complications in the long run, and his wasn't a life made for emotional attachments. But he didn't see any harm in bringing this one young woman out of her protective shell and making her enjoy her trip. He had a feeling he wouldn't have to worry much about getting too close to her, for she wouldn't let him.

"Watch it, Hoffman, next thing you know you'll actually be caring about her," he scolded himself, then headed toward the snack bar. An ice cream cone was just what he needed to clear his brain and get that pretty, sullen tourist off his mind.

It was late that afternoon when the boat docked at Koblenz and the tour group left the boat for the bus. Sandy had spent the intervening hours only half seeing the scenery. She wasn't sure why she had behaved the way she had toward Rick, but on reflection she felt it was the right thing to do. She hadn't had the time she needed to heal from her last broken heart. It wouldn't do to let her overactive imagination develop any romantic fantasies around the gorgeous tour guide. That could only hurt her, and she couldn't bear to be hurt again.

She boarded the bus with the large family, making a point to be talking to the mother so she could avoid speaking to Rick. Again she took the window seat next to Justin, who pulled out his computer game before the bus began to move. Soon Sandy was once again surrounded by a flurry of beeps and whistles. She wondered if he had played with the toy during the whole cruise, or if he had actually looked at a castle or two. Not that she had seen much herself other than the things Rick had pointed out to her. She knew she shouldn't have let her mother talk her into taking this trip. Her heart just wasn't in it.

She leaned her head against the window and watched the countryside fly by, her thoughts racing almost as fast as the bus on the Autobahn. Despite her previous decision that avoiding any involvement with Rick was the right thing, she still couldn't stop thinking about him. In the reflection in the bus window her head rested against she could see him making his way up and down the aisle of the bus, stopping to chat with the tourists. His friendly behavior hadn't been limited to her. He could make anyone smile or laugh, and his efforts seemed genuine. She wondered what could make a man that genial come to success in a profession in which all relationships were limited to a matter of weeks. She shifted a bit in her seat so she could watch the real Rick, rather than just the image. Lulled by the motion of the bus, she drifted off to sleep, still gazing at Rick.

The last conscious thought in her mind was that if she weren't careful she could fall head over heels in love with Richard Hoffman, and the good-byes when the tour ended would be too painful to bear.

Chapter Three

When Sandy woke, it seemed as if they hadn't gone anywhere. They were still on a road that ran along the top of a deep river valley whose sides were covered with vineyards. Rubbing her eyes, Sandy muttered, "Where are we now?"

Without taking his eyes from his game, Justin shrugged. "I dunno," he said, then punctuated it with an exultant, "Yes!" Sandy guessed he must have done something good in his game.

Justin's mother leaned across the aisle. "I'm really not sure where we are, but I think we're near a different river—Mozle something."

Her theory was confirmed when Rick's voice came over the loudspeaker a couple of seconds later. "Ladies and gentlemen," he said, "Today you've received the deluxe German river tour. After our Rhine cruise we are now traveling along the Moselle. In a few moments we will stop at our inn for tonight. I'm sure you romantic types—" Sandy could feel his gaze across the length of the bus when he said that "—will enjoy this inn, because it's in a remodeled castle.'' The bus erupted with oohs and ahs of interest, and Rick continued, ''Upon our arrival we will have a light supper. I hope you ate well during the cruise and enjoyed some of the fine cuisine offered on the German Rhine Line's ships.''

Sandy had only had an ice cream cone from the ship's snack bar, and hadn't really felt like eating even that. Now at the mention of a meal her stomach began to remind her of food. Fortunately, Rick was true to his word and they arrived at the inn within fifteen minutes.

It wasn't soon enough for Sandy, whose patience was wearing thin. Earlier in the day she had been able to tolerate the constant computer game noise, but now after the beeps and buzzes had insinuated themselves into her sleep, and as her empty stomach made her even more grouchy, it was more than she could bear. By the time they reached the inn she had sworn never to have children, and if she did she would never give them computer games.

Her weariness and bad temper must have shown in her face, for as she got off the bus Rick asked her, ''Are you sure you don't want to sit with me?''

One look at the gentle concern in his eyes was enough to make her patience return full-fold. ''Are you kidding? There's just something about being with a child to enable me to see Europe through a child's eyes, with all the wonder and innocence,'' she said with an airy brightness she didn't feel. She took her room key from him and went to pick up her bags, vowing to herself that she would stuff her ears with cotton for the rest of the trip. As she went upstairs she wondered again how much Justin was seeing. He could probably stand to look at Europe through a child's eyes himself.

Sandy was too hungry to waste time unpacking. She hung up her clothes for the next day, splashed her face with cold water and brushed her hair. Rick's words about seeing her without makeup came back to her and she quickly added a touch of lipstick before hurrying down to the dining room.

She was one of the first there, but she was soon joined by the Williamson twins. Sandy greeted them, but didn't stop eating to make conversation. The meal was simple but filling, a mix of fresh fruit, bread, sausage and cheese. As she ate, Sandy listened to the two sisters talk. They were arguing over the castles they had seen along the way. Ida favored the craggy ruins while Inez thought they were eyesores and should be destroyed. When they asked her opinion, Sandy had to quickly swallow a mouthful of bread and cheese.

"Those castles are a part of history. They have their own kind of beauty," she told them. "But to be honest, my favorite was the one on the island in the middle of the river."

"Well, yes," Inez said. "I'm sure your head is full of those romantic notions. I should have known, considering the upbringing you must have had."

Sandy cringed at the veiled reference to her mother.

She of all people knew she couldn't have turned out normal with a mother whose idea of work was lounging on a sofa, wearing silk pajamas and dictating romance novels that always ended happily. Maybe what she had needed was a grim dose of reality, a love affair that didn't have a happy ending. That was one way of looking at it, she mused. Had Gregory's rejection of her been really all that bad, or had it just been a cruel contrast to all her ideals?

Raised voices from the two sisters brought her back to the present. The Williamsons were now arguing over which Penelope Harrison book was their favorite. Sandy couldn't take that with her already frazzled nerves, so she excused herself from the table and left the dining room. She paused in the front parlour to look out the window. Even though it was fairly late in the evening, it was still light outside. Having lived most of her life in more southern latitudes, these incredibly long summer days held a certain magic for her. On an impulse she slipped outside for a short walk.

The view from the front of the inn was breathtaking. The sides of the steeply sloped river valley were covered in grape vines. Across the valley she could see a small village nestled between the river and the vineyard. In the distance the graceful arc of a bridge spanned the chasm, and below it all was the river, winding like a great silver snake through the valley. Drawn by the spectacle before her, she walked toward the vineyard until she saw a little path winding down the slope. With a glance back at the old castle, she began to pick her way carefully down the path.

As she walked, her mind cleared for the first time in weeks. The hurt and anger had ebbed and she could almost feel her emotional equilibrium returning. If only she could stay here for the rest of the trip and not have to travel the rest of the way around Germany, dealing with bratty kids, cantankerous old women and the emotional tumult caused by a certain tour guide.

The sound of a foot on gravel startled her out of her reflective mood. She whirled to look behind her, and there, as if summoned by her thoughts of him, was Rick.

"How dare you follow me!" she lashed at him, shaken somewhat at being caught thinking of him. "I needed to be alone," she added more softly.

"Yes, you've made that very clear," he replied, his voice cool and calm, in contrast to the storm raging in his blue eyes. "But this time I thought I had better stick with you. Whether you know it or not, you've gone quite a distance. You can hardly see the inn from here, and I didn't want you to get lost. It's also not safe for a woman to be wandering by herself at this time of the evening, no matter where you are. You are my responsibility and I do like to take precautions."

Sandy noticed that it was much darker now than it had been when she set out. She wondered how long she had been walking, and how long he had been following. She turned back around without a word and continued walking, her mood remaining surprisingly peaceful following her brief outburst, despite Rick's presence.

He was the first to break the silence after they had walked for several minutes. "What was it that hurt you so badly?" he asked abruptly in that same perfectly even voice he had used earlier.

She froze, her heart suddenly pounding wildly. He was too perceptive for her own comfort. When she had calmed herself sufficiently to speak without betraying her true feelings, she turned to face him and said lightly, "What do you mean by that?"

He regarded her with those stormy eyes before saying softly, "If you ever decide you want to talk about it, I'm here." Then his mouth quirked in that sardonic way of his and he added, "After all, it is my job to see to it that everyone is happy." His eyes were still serious, despite his light tone. He maintained eye contact with her for another moment, then turned and walked away, back toward the inn.

She noticed then that he had managed to steer her down another path that led back to the inn, and they were almost there. She watched his retreating back until he entered the front door. Only when he disappeared was she able to let out the breath she hadn't been aware she had been holding since he had first made that intense eye contact with her. She took a couple of steadying breaths to chase that sensation from her before she, too, began to make her way back.

The sun had gone down completely by the time she got to her room. Suddenly dead tired, she began to get ready for bed, but she couldn't calm her now-turbulent thoughts enough to sleep. She got up and opened the shutters, then stood in the window, staring out into the night at the lights on the river below and in the star-filled sky above. The night air caressing her face had the effect of returning her to her previous calm emotional state, but she was still too restless mentally to sleep.

Instead she pulled out her laptop computer and started to write up notes of what she'd seen that day, just in case her mother might want to use it as background material. As she mentally ran through the castles she had seen that day, she remembered her storybook fantasy about a kidnapped princess held by the robber baron. That would make a good story, she thought, then remembered Rick's question of whether she had tried to write anything of her own. With a burst of enthusiasm she closed her research file and opened a new one. This would be her own story, and this was her opportunity to write it.

This was also her opportunity to create a true storybook hero, one who would never dump his lady without warning. That gave her something to start with. She curled up in a chair by the open window with the computer in her lap and wrote until late in the night.

Sandy was awakened the next morning by the sound of a boat whistle that came into her room through the still-open window. She lay in bed for a moment, luxuriating in the feel of the soft sheets and the warm down comforter. The air in her room was cool and it felt good to stay in bed. She glanced around the room at the antique furniture and intricate tapestries that hung on the walls. The calls of birds and the distant hum of traffic were the only interruptions to the stillness. Again, she wished she could stay here for the rest of the trip and not have to face Rick again. She was afraid if he got to know her much better he would be able to see straight through her.

Her wish was not to be, for in the next moment there came a great pounding on her door. "Rise and shine, sleepyhead," Rick's voice boomed. "We've got a busy day ahead and you don't want to miss breakfast."

Sandy groaned and reached for her watch on the bedside table. It was late. She must have overslept after the previous evening's insomnia. "Sandy, are you in there?" came Rick's voice again.

She didn't want him standing out there all morning, so she answered, "Yes, I'm in here, and I'm awake. I'll be ready for breakfast in a minute."

"Make it quick," was his reply, then Sandy could hear his footsteps echoing down the hall. She jumped out of bed and hurried to the bathroom for a quick shower, then brushed her hair, put on some lipstick and dressed in a pair of blue jeans and a blouse. Remembering the cool temperature, she threw a sweater over her shoulders before heading for the dining room.

Rick was there waiting for her. "It's about time," he said.

"Sorry. I must have overslept."

"You didn't have any trouble getting to sleep last night, I hope."

He can see right through me, she thought, but she forced a smile and replied, "Oh no, not at all. I slept very well, thank you."

He arched an eyebrow at her. "That's good to know." He escorted her to a table, then sat beside her.

"Haven't you eaten yet?" she asked him.

"No, I was too busy getting some slugabeds up. And I was saving myself for you."

"Don't starve yourself for me," she said lightly. "We all need you at full strength."

In reply, he handed her the bread basket. Inside were the ubiquitous hard rolls. She sighed and took one, for she didn't think there was a bakery within walking distance here. Gingerly, she picked up her knife and made an attempt at slicing the roll open, but only succeeded in showering herself with crumbs. Rick laughed softly, but made no attempt to help. That was all the incentive she needed to master this evil excuse for breakfast food. With a glare at Rick she stabbed her knife deep into the heart of the roll, then tore it apart.

"Whew, remind me not to get in your way if you have a knife in your hand before you've had your first cup of coffee," he teased her.

Sandy blushed furiously, but in a way she was relieved. She could handle it when he was baiting her and they were engaging in verbal duels. As long as he was like this she didn't have to worry too much about her feelings getting out of control. She just hoped he didn't show his more gentle side again.

After everyone had eaten breakfast and packed, they began to load the bus again. As the baggage was being stowed under the bus, Rick told the assembled group, "This morning we will go to Trier, a German city known for its Roman ruins. Then we'll drive to Paris. We should arrive there early this evening. Now, if you would care to begin boarding the bus, we can get on our way."

As Sandy made her way toward the bus she fought down a sigh of resignation. Another day trapped with a ten-year-old. Ever-perceptive Rick noticed her gloomy look.

"What's the matter?" he asked. "Do you have some sort of prejudice against Roman ruins? Or is it the thought of Paris that disgusts you? Or maybe it's sitting next to the Nintendo champion of the world for another day?"

"The Nintendo champion."

"You could always sit with me."

"The lesser of two evils?" she asked, raising one eyebrow sardonically.

"Evil? Me? You don't have anything to be afraid of from me. I don't even own a computer game. I think you're just afraid you won't have anything to complain about. Maybe you want to be miserable."

Sandy rolled her eyes and tried to look insulted, but the effect was ruined when Mrs. Forester, who was waiting behind Sandy, chided Rick, "Young man, I think you should concentrate on doing your job rather than annoying this young lady." With a wink at Rick she pushed her way between them, and pulling her husband behind her, she boarded the bus.

Sandy had to fight hard not to laugh, but it proved to be too much of an effort for her. Tears streaming down her cheeks, she finally burst out in hysterical giggles. Rick glared at her, his attempt at looking angry betrayed by the twinkle in his eyes. "I think she may be right," he said when Sandy gained control of her laughter. "Maybe I am neglecting my job. So, to make amends I will rescue you from several hours of Nintendo noise by making you sit with me."

Sandy regarded him carefully for a moment, then, hardly believing what she was doing, said, "After lunch."

"If you insist." He stuck out his hand. "Deal?"

She took his hand and shook it as firmly as she could. "Deal." They stood for a moment, hand in hand, until Sandy finally let go. She had to, or risk losing her composure. Once again the electric sensation of his touch had startled her. "I'd better take my seat," she gasped quickly, then ran up the steps of the bus. He stood looking up at the bus for a few seconds more, then got on and took his own seat.

Sandy was glad the drive to Trier was short, because Justin again played his game through the whole trip. In an attempt to shut out the annoyance, she turned toward the window and rested her head against the back of the seat. From that position she watched the world go by and thought about Rick.

She was beginning to wonder if he was indeed just casually flirting or if there was something more. She really wasn't sure which she wanted. The gentleness in his offer of the night before to listen if she needed it belied his more usual sarcasm. She guessed at untold depths to the handsome tour guide, and she found herself wanting to know more. The hint of danger at being drawn too deeply into another relationship so soon after one had ended whispered at the back of her mind, but she told herself that with his apparent attitude and his chosen profession he probably wasn't looking for any kind of committed relationship. As long as she was aware of that she should be all right. Besides, she didn't want any kind of commitment herself right now. A little flirtation with Rick might be just what she needed to put Gregory well and truly behind her.

Fortunately for Sandy's nerves, the drive to Trier wasn't long. The bus came to a stop in front of a massive black stone fortress. Sandy stared out the window at it in awe until the bus was almost empty. Rick was waiting for her when she got off the bus. She gave him a bright smile, bright enough to shock him into silence. She pretended not to notice his discomposure and said, ''Who gets the honor of showing us the sights today?''

He gave her a cocky grin and said, ''Today you

don't have to wait for the English translation. The whole group gets the Hoffman deluxe tour guided by yours truly.''

"Oh, are you such an expert?''

"I've been here hundreds of times. I know it like the back of my own hand.''

"That sounds promising. I'm looking forward to it.''

He frowned slightly. "What's wrong with you?'' he asked.

"What?'' she asked sweetly.

"You're actually being friendly to me, without me having to try. That's not like you.''

"And how do you know what I'm like?''

"From what I've seen in the couple of days I've known you, you're reserved, stand-offish, moody and a loner. You warm up a little after I hit you with my best efforts, but we have to start from square one the next time we talk. For all I know, that's what you're like.''

"Why do you put in so much effort on me if you think I'm reserved, moody and stand-offish?''

He shrugged and seemed to grope for words. "I hate to be around depressed people, so I do what I can to cheer them up,'' he finally said. "And once you loosen up a bit you can be fun. Like now, for instance. You keep me on my toes.''

She feigned innocence. "Do I? Well, I guess I just needed someone to expend a little effort for me.''

"Glad to oblige.'' He offered her his arm, "Now,

if you would care to join me for a brief tour of this lovely city . . .''

She declined the arm with a shake of her head and said, ''I'd be glad to join you, but I'll just stick with the rest of the group.''

''Be that way, but you're the one missing out.''

''I know, but we don't want people to talk, now do we?''

He gave a deep, exaggerated sigh. ''Woman, you really want to make me work, don't you?''

She tossed her hair in what she hoped looked like a casual movement. ''I think I'm worth a little effort.''

He was prevented from replying to that by the rest of the group crowding around them. With a glance at the group, he took a deep breath and instantly transformed into the tour guide once more. ''Many of the sights we've seen in the past couple of days are from medieval times or later, but Trier was once a great Roman city. It was from Trier that the Caesars ruled the western part of their empire, from Spain to Britain. One legacy of that rule stands behind me. The Porta Negra, or Black Gate, was once the northern gate to the city. In Roman times there was a wall around the city and there were four more gates like this one.''

As Sandy watched him go through his well-practiced speech, she couldn't help but be impressed. He knew his subject, even if he did give the air that he had done this one too many times before. She soon lost track of his actual words and simply followed him, studying him closely for some clue as to the kind of man he really was.

He was intelligent, that much was obvious in his eyes. There was a depth there she couldn't comprehend. She studied his features, the sculpted cheekbones, the strong jaw and determined chin. A slight breeze blew his blond hair across his forehead. He could have fit into any group of natives she had seen thus far on the trip. He didn't seem to notice her perusal, and for that she was grateful. She didn't want to have to explain herself.

By this time, he had led them up into the massive stone gate and was telling them they could take a few minutes to climb the stairs to the upper level and look out over the city. Sandy was climbing the worn stone steps, cautious of the indented areas where thousands of feet had trod for more than a thousand years, when Rick came up behind her. She started, feeling a bit guilty at thinking about him, but he caught her with a strong hand at her elbow.

Still holding her arm, he asked her, "Have you learned anything so far?" She felt his voice resonate within her body and echo off the close walls of the stairwell.

"I'm afraid I'm hopelessly lost," she told him, hoping her voice didn't give away her feelings. "I was too busy looking around to catch all those names and dates."

He shook his head and tsk-tsked her, "That's too

bad. You were aware there is a test over the tour so far tonight?''

"If there is, I'm sunk. I think I remember a couple of your stories from yesterday, but as I said, I have a lousy memory for dates. I may be able to describe everything we see, though.''

He cocked his head to one side in an imitation of deep thought, then said, ''I guess that will have to do. Now, shall we continue our climb?'' He continued to hold her arm as they climbed to the top of the stairs.

The view from the top of the fortress was breathtaking, but not as breathtaking as the presence of the man who stood at her side. She knew she shouldn't be letting him affect her like this, but as long as she was thinking of Rick, she wasn't thinking of Gregory, and she wasn't hurting.

"I can just imagine Roman soldiers looking out from here, watching for attacks from the conquered tribes,'' she murmured softly. "I wonder what kind of view they saw.''

"Probably not a parking garage. There you go with those romantic notions of yours.''

"I can't help it if I have a vivid imagination,'' she said archly.

"Right. Now, if you'll excuse me, I ought to round up the group so we can get on with this tour.'' He walked off and started finding the other members of their group and herding them down the stairs. Sandy followed them down the stairs and out the other side of the building, into the old town and then into the marketplace.

Here the buildings looked storybook medieval, with no hint of the city's Roman influence. Rick was saying something to that effect, listing the dates the gabled and half-timbered buildings were built. Sandy was too busy glancing around the marketplace, looking at the people and the buildings. Looking back over her shoulder at the black fortress looming over the old town, she had a sense of history she had never noticed in her hometown of Dallas, where an old building was built at the turn of the century. These buildings dated at the latest from the fifteenth century. Standing in that old marketplace she felt linked to fate and history, and glancing back at Rick she felt that same sense of fate. It made her heart pound harder and her pulse quicken. As she looked at him, he glanced in her direction and their eyes met. For a moment they seemed suspended in time and place as the centuries whirled by.

A question from Mr. Forester brought Rick back to his senses. He asked the older man to repeat the question, then paused to think for a second or two to come up with the answer. Sandy just stared at the cobblestones beneath her feet, afraid that she might meet Rick's eyes again. That moment had made her afraid that she could never convince herself that she was capable of keeping things light between them. She longed for him to tease her or start an argument, and she regretted her promise to sit with him on the long drive to Paris.

The unexpected eye contact had astonished Rick just as much as it had Sandy. Only his long practice in giving this tour had enabled him to keep his composure. He could describe most of Europe in his sleep, and there had been many a sleepless night when he felt he had. His mouth went on autopilot while his mind raced. He hadn't been prepared for the way a simple eye contact could affect him. Up until now he would have said he was immune to the effects of a glance from a girl, so this was an unusual experience for him. He didn't know why he was feeling this way. Maybe it was compassion for the hurt in her that was too deep to talk about. Perhaps it was intrigue at finding a woman who challenged him. Whatever it was, he felt something important had just happened, and Richard Hoffman was a man who followed his feelings. That was what had gotten him where he was today.

He finished his description of the market area, then led the group down a couple of side streets back to the bus so they could visit the ancient Roman amphitheater and the baths. At the bus he stopped Sandy as she began to climb the steps. "Is our deal still on?" he asked, as casually as he could.

She gave him a smile that didn't touch her eyes. "We haven't had lunch yet." There was a slight catch in her voice.

"Boy, you do drive a hard bargain." He followed her onto the bus and took his own seat behind the driver, shaking his head in disgust. Maybe that moment back in the marketplace was just a fluke after all. He didn't need a prickly, overly sensitive woman. But he wondered what it was that had hurt her. He had a feeling it was a man, and he wanted to know what kind of man could hurt a romantic dreamer like Sandy enough to turn her bitter. He hoped he somehow could have the chance to heal her.

Chapter Four

Sandy was disappointed in the Roman baths. Although she should have known better she was expecting marble tiles and graceful columns. What she saw instead were crumbling stone walls behind wire fences. The amphitheater was no better. As hard as she tried, she couldn't conjure up images of gladiators or actors performing for the crowds of Roman soldiers. It was just decaying rock. While the rest of the group prowled the amphitheater, she just stood in its center, gazing up at where rows of seats had been centuries before.

When she saw Rick approaching, she forced her mouth into a smile. All she needed now was his sympathy and she'd burst into tears. Instead she laughed and said, "It's hard to believe we've come all this way to look at some old rocks."

"Old rocks? This is history!" He regarded her quizzically. "Now wait a minute. Aren't you the hopeless romantic who sees a story in everything?"

"Most of the time. But it's hard to see much in this. Maybe I'm just more interested in fairy tales."

"We'll be in Paris this evening. That should be more to your liking."

She sighed, then said, "I hope so."

"Trust me, Paris will be everything you expected, and more."

"Spoken like a true tour guide."

"Of course. Now if you'll excuse me . . ." He put two fingers to his lips and gave a loud whistle, then waved his arm over his head in a signal for the group to gather. "It's time for lunch," he explained to a startled Sandy, whose ears were still ringing.

After a quick lunch at an ancient inn, they boarded the bus to make the trip to Paris. Her heart pounding inexplicably, Sandy took the window seat just behind the driver. Rick raised an eyebrow at her when he got on after all the other passengers. "So, you are a woman of your word," he said, taking the seat next to her.

"Of course. You thought otherwise?"

"No, but I scarcely dared hope."

She had to smile at the earnest way he said that. She realized now why she found herself seeking out his company: he made her smile, and smiles had been too few for her lately. She settled herself in the corner between the seat and the window so she could look at him. As the bus began to move she said, "So, Richard Hoffman, tell me about yourself." The boldness of the question shocked even her. It wasn't like Sandy Harrison to say something like that.

Rick worried his lower lip with his teeth and frowned

for a moment. Sandy was just about to withdraw the question when he said, ''What do you want to know?''

She shrugged. ''Oh, I don't know. How did you learn to speak like a native?''

''I studied modern languages in college, and it helps that I've been here quite a while. I think I've spent close to 20 years in Europe.''

She took another look at him. He couldn't be older than thirty, so she didn't see how he could have been working here for so long. Before she could ask, he explained, ''My dad was in the Army and I spent much of my childhood overseas. After college I came back.'' He glanced her way, then said, ''That's more than I know about you.''

''True, but now it's your turn. Why did you come back here after college?''

''I really don't know. I guess I'm just kind of rootless, and I had as many attachments over here as I had anywhere else. It was sort of the thing to do right after college. You know, pack some things in a backpack and head out across a different continent, relying on your wits to survive.''

Sandy didn't know. She would never have dared try something like that when she had finished college. She had just continued working for her mother and dating good-old Gregory, planning a wedding that was never to happen. But she didn't want to tell Rick this, so she just nodded. ''Why did you stay?'' she asked.

''It just sort of happened. I ran into someone who needed a guide. I spoke the language and knew the place. I also knew Americans. I turned out to be good at it, ended up with a permanent job and eventually started my own company.''

''You own the company?''

''Yes, didn't you know?''

She shook her head. ''I had no idea.''

''It was in the brochure. I would have thought with your caution you would have found out everything you could before you committed to the tour.''

''I didn't have much of a choice. My mother bought the tour and gave it to me as a surprise. I don't even have any idea where we're going.''

He smiled. ''That's a nice gift. I'm flattered.'' He tilted his head at her, then said, ''Now it's your turn.''

''My turn?''

''To tell me something about yourself. All I know is that your mother writes and you're the business end of the operation, yet you're a hopeless romantic.''

''There's not much more to say.''

''Come on, your life can't have been that boring. Where are you from? Where did you go to school?''

''I'm from Dallas and I went to school at a small private college in town.''

They had both slipped down in their seats and sat with their heads together and kept their voices soft, so as to shut out the rest of the bus and maintain some degree of privacy. As their conversation grew more intimate, they drew even closer together until they were close to touching.

"What about your parents?" she asked him. "What do they think about you being away all this time?"

"It's not like I've been living in exile. I go back for visits occasionally, and they're over here frequently. My mother is German, so they come visit her relatives."

That explained his proficiency in the language, she thought. She was afraid of the question that would naturally follow, and she didn't want to talk about her father.

He either sensed her discomfort or was uncomfortable himself, for his next question was a gentle non-sequitur. "What kind of music do you like?"

"I don't really know. I just like music in general."

"What about jazz?"

"Jazz is nice."

"I know this great little club in Paris that has the best jazz I've ever heard."

"Mmm. Sounds nice." They were even closer together now, their voices down to husky purrs, his hair tickling her forehead as he leaned close to her. It was as though nothing existed outside their shared bus seat.

Then the real world broke in abruptly when the bus stopped. The driver said something to Rick, who sat up quickly and picked up his microphone. "Ladies and gentlemen," he announced. "We're at the French border now. You may want to have your passports handy." He put the microphone back in its holder and opened the bus door, then got up and went down the steps to meet the border guard.

A rapid conversation in French ensued, Rick looking his most charming and genial, the guard gradually warming to him. Sandy was impressed. She wondered how many languages the guide spoke. So far he had demonstrated fluency in two besides English. The sound of his voice in French sent shivers up her spine. The two men outside the bus shook hands, then the guard went back to his booth and Rick got back on the bus. He said something in German to the driver and settled back in his seat.

"Well, that was easier than I thought," he said. "It helps that I'm well-known there."

"Don't tell me they play favorites."

"Of course they do. But don't tell anyone."

She nodded and shifted in her seat, but the spell that had grown between them had been broken. She couldn't bring herself to ask him another personal question, and she would be relieved not to have to answer another from him. "How long 'til we get to Paris?" she asked, just to break the silence.

He grinned. "You sound like my sister used to when she was a kid." He changed his voice to a perfect imitation of an impatient child, "Mom, how much longer? When will we get there? Are we almost there yet?"

"Well?" she prodded when she had managed to contain her laughter.

"Well what?"

"How much longer?"

"Oh, about three or four hours."

She nodded in acknowledgement, then leaned against the window. ''I hope you don't think I'm hopelessly rude, but I'm going to fall asleep on you.''

''Go right ahead,'' he told her, and he watched her as she closed her eyes. It took less than a minute before the motion of the bus had lulled her into a deep sleep.

Rick watched her sleep, amazed at the transformation unconsciousness wrought. She lost that wounded, defensive look and instead looked innocent, almost angelic. Her long, dark eyelashes rested against her cheeks and her silky brown hair spread out over her shoulders. Her full lips were slightly parted, and he had to draw himself back from their moist invitation. She seemed too fragile to touch. At that moment he would have defended her from anything.

That thought was a revelation to him, for he had never felt that way before. He didn't know what it was about this girl that had touched him so. There was her unselfconscious prettiness, the vulnerability that lay sheltered behind a host of witty remarks, the wide-eyed wonder with which she saw the world and the way she had made him look at things in a new way. It wasn't what he usually looked for in a short flirtation, but he was enjoying himself. Getting along with her was getting surprisingly easy. Her behavior to him today had been promising. He hadn't had to work very hard to keep her talking, and she had even instigated a conversation or two. He shifted position so he could rest his cheek against the back of his seat and watch her sleep, memorizing every detail of her face.

Sandy woke a little more than an hour later. Rick's seat was empty, but when she sat up and craned her neck she could see him walking down the bus aisle, answering questions and talking with the tourists. She watched him make his way toward the front of the bus, admiring his easy confidence with people. She wished she could be that at ease and that good at making conversation. She smiled as he tried in vain to get some kind of reaction out of Justin, then gave up and came back to the front of the bus.

"Must have been a good nap," as he took his seat next to her.

"Yes, it was nice," was all she said.

"Good."

They settled into a silence, but it wasn't uncomfortable. She just didn't feel the need to speak. She hadn't felt this comfortable with a man in her life. A warning signal went off in her brain, but she chose to ignore it. There was no harm in making a new friend, was there?

It was early evening when they arrived in Paris. Sandy gazed out the bus window, trying to drink in every sight. She had always dreamed of coming here. Paris had beckoned to her as a city of mystery, adventure and romance. Now she wondered if it would be as wonderful without the promise of love. She shoved the threatening depression to the back of her mind and tried to concentrate on the details as the bus drove down wide avenues and narrow lanes to the hotel.

When the bus came to a stop, all the passengers stood up and stretched wearily. Before he opened the door and allowed the passengers off, Rick picked up the microphone and announced, ''We will have dinner in about thirty minutes. After that the evening is your own.'' He then opened the door and the travellers exited slowly. Sandy and Rick both waited until the end before getting off.

The driver had exited through his own side door and was already unloading luggage. Sandy collected her tapestried bags, got her room key from Rick, who had checked them all in, and went up to her room. She was desperate to wash her face and brush her teeth. After sleeping on the bus she felt like rats had nested all over her body. When she saw the luxurious bathroom she decided to take a shower instead.

Thirty minutes later she had put on a wrinkle-proof knit dress, applied fresh makeup and dried her hair, leaving it loose around her shoulders. She was working on the finishing touches when there was a knock at her door. She got up from the dressing table and opened the door to find Rick, who had also changed clothes. ''Are you ready for dinner?'' he asked.

''I was just about to go down,'' she said.

''Then, would you care to join me?'' He offered her his arm.

She smiled, chasing the nagging worries to the back

of her mind. After all, she was in Paris, and what was Paris without a handsome, romantic man? If it weren't for Rick the memories of Gregory threatened to come flooding in, and she couldn't take that. She took Rick's arm and let him lead her to the dining room.

In contrast to the dining rooms she had seen thus far on the trip, this one looked like an elegant restaurant. Candlelight flickered on silver, china and snowy linen. He noticed her admiring gaze and said, ''Now you see where the bulk of your mother's money went on this tour. I figure if you're going to go to Paris you might as well do it in style.''

She had to agree with him. A brief thought of what a honeymoon with Gregory might have been like here crossed her mind, but she banished it. She was here and she was going to enjoy herself.

Rick escorted her to a table for two. She noticed that instead of the larger group tables that had been in previous places there were smaller, more intimate arrangements here. She was grateful to have Rick with her, because otherwise she might have felt very much alone. She gave him her most sparkling smile as he held her chair for her, then took his own seat. The other guests began to come into the dining room. They all glanced at Sandy and Rick, and she began to feel a bit self conscious about being with him.

She shook off the last of her doubts and looked across the table into his eyes. Her imaginative mind was already writing this scene. Except in her book it would take place in a medieval banquet hall between a princess and a knight, and their story would end happily ever after, while this would just end. No hurt, no strong feelings, just memories of a good time. The waiter came to serve the soup course and they both began to eat, stopping only for occasional small talk.

Soon after they finished dessert, a dance band began to play in the hotel lounge next door to the dining room. Sounds of soft jazz wafted into the dining room. Rick smiled at Sandy and said, "Remember that nice little jazz club I told you about?"

Sandy nodded. "Is this it?"

"No, but I think we need to warm up. Do you dance?"

"Not well."

"Good. Neither do I. Shall we?"

She bit her lip, torn between her desire to have a good time and her fear of getting any closer to Rick. The pause was too long for him. "Come on, are you going to make me beg in public? I don't often get the chance to go dancing, so please don't deprive me."

She gave a deep sigh of resignation. "Okay, okay, you win. But trust me, you'll be sorry and your feet will hate you for it."

He glanced at her feet as she stood up, then said, "It looks like I'm pretty safe. No spiked heels." He took her hand and half dragged her out of the dining room and into the lounge.

The club was just beginning to fill up when they got there. "Good," Rick remarked. "We'll have more room to practice in."

"And there will be fewer people to watch us make fools of ourselves," Sandy added.

The band finished the first number and started another. Rick led Sandy onto the dance floor and took her awkwardly in his arms in the classic ballroom dancing position. "You do know what you're doing," she accused him.

"My mother made me take a dance class when I was a kid. I remember the basics, but there's not much polish. Now hush, I need to find the rhythm." He began counting the beat under his breath, then stepped forward. Sandy followed his lead. "We'll just keep it simple for a while, shall we?" he murmured as he guided her around the floor.

After the first turn around the floor Sandy could feel him relax. His hold on her became more secure and he began to lead with more confidence. "See, this isn't as difficult as we thought. I haven't stepped on you yet," he said with a grin. His good humor was so contagious that Sandy relaxed as well. She risked a glance at his face, but he was looking over her shoulder, concentrating carefully on maneuvering around the dance floor without bumping into another couple.

The song ended and the band swung into a faster number. "Think we can handle this one?" Rick asked.

"Why not? Lead on."

"Okay, here goes." Once they fell into the rhythm of the song they began to move as one, able to anticipate each other's moves. Suddenly he said, "Now that we've got the hang of that, let's try something a little fancier.'' He spun Sandy into a quick turn and she came back breathless into his arms. ''You pick this up quickly,'' he commented.

''You're a good teacher,'' she said. He grinned and spun her around again and again. She was breathless by the time the song ended, but when the band eased into a slower number, Rick didn't give her the option of sitting down. He simply pulled her closer and kept dancing.

Sandy let the music carry her away as she settled into the flow of the dance and began to concentrate instead on the man who held her. The feel of his hand on her back seemed to burn its way through her dress and onto her skin. As he held her close to him she could feel the beating of his heart. She wasn't the only one who was breathless at the end of that dance.

When the music ended they both stepped away from each other, suddenly awkward. In the dim lights of the room, Sandy thought she could see a flush come over his fair skin, rising from his neck to his hairline. She was afraid to meet his eyes, for fear he could read in them the thoughts she had just had. She had a sudden urge to get away immediately, before she made a mistake she knew she'd regret.

''That was fun,'' she told him, straining to look carefree and happy. ''Now I'm looking forward to that little jazz club of yours, but for now I really want to get to work. I started writing something last night and I'd like to finish at least an outline before I get home.''

He didn't meet her eyes when he replied, ''So you

did decide to write something of your own. Good luck. I hope it goes well. I'll see you tomorrow morning.'' Then that familiar, charming grin spread over his face, and he added, "Don't stay up too late working. Tomorrow's going to be a busy day of sightseeing.'' He walked with her to the elevator and made a move as if to join her and walk her to her room, but stepped back as she got on the elevator. "Good night. Sleep well.'' Then the door closed between them and she was left alone.

Rick watched the elevator door close, then kicked at the large potted plant that sat between the two elevators. He shoved his hands deep into his pockets and stalked back into the lobby. "Good job, Hoffman,'' he muttered to himself. "Scare her, why don't you. Could you have pushed just a bit harder?'' He shook his head in disgust. Why was he so caught up in this girl anyway? He watched the Foresters stroll through the lobby, hand in hand, then sighed. "Admit it,'' he told himself. "She's just the first girl you couldn't sweep off her feet with your smile, and you can't stand that. She's just another tourist and after next week you'll never see her again.'' He wasn't very convincing.

A shrill voice calling his name shocked him out of his self-chastisement. "Yoo hoo, Mr. Hoffman!'' He glanced to his right and saw Ida Williamson. "Oh, no!'' he groaned and rolled his eyes, then instantly put on his charming tour guide face.

"Good evening, Miss Williamson. How are you?"

"Oh, I'm just peachy. Inez and I were going to sit here and watch people come and go. We want to be able to describe all these Parisians to the folks back home."

A sudden urge to laugh seized him, but he fought for and maintained control. "Well, Miss Williamson, if you really want to see Parisians you might want to find a cafe or club away from the hotel. Not many locals frequent hotels."

She gasped and shook her head. "No, we wouldn't dare leave the hotel after dark. It just isn't safe for two ladies to go out by ourselves at night. You know, big cities are all full of criminals."

The hint in her voice was obvious, and normally Rick would have been glad to oblige even two funny old women like these, but tonight he wasn't in the mood. "There are plenty of Parisians out in the daytime, too," he told her. "You'll see some tomorrow."

Ida didn't give up so easily. "Do you have plans for the evening, Mr. Hoffman?"

He shook his head wearily. "No, I'm going to turn in early. Remember, this is all work for me."

Ida giggled and batted her eyes at him like she was a teenager at her first cotillion. "What? A handsome young man like you alone in Paris? Come now, what about that Miss Harrison? She's pretty enough, even if she is a mousy little thing, but she does seem to fancy you a bit."

He was saved from having to reply to that by Inez,

who came out of the powder room to join her sister. Before she could join in the conversation, he excused himself and turned back toward the elevators. In the elevator going up he thought, "What about that Miss Harrison? She's pretty, not as mousy as she would like people to think and she keeps me guessing. She's also nursing a big hurt and has no need for a guy like me." That settled in his mind, he got off the elevator and went to his room. As he unlocked the door, an unbidden thought crossed his mind. "But what if I need her?"

Chapter Five

It was several minutes after Sandy got back to her room before she was able to do anything but collapse in the big armchair that sat beside the bed. She knew she shouldn't be reacting like this to a simple dance, but her legs were shaking and she had a hollow feeling in her stomach. It couldn't be just attraction, for she had never really felt that with Gregory, and she had loved him enough to want to marry him. This was different. Probably just a rebound attraction, she mused. This was a good transition for her. She could enjoy herself with a man who held no future for her, then she could return to Dallas and look Gregory in the eye without wanting to either cry or hit him.

She pulled out the computer again and looked over what she had written—could it just have been last night? She was pleased with what she saw. The beginnings of the story showed promise. There was danger, excitement, enchantment, and just a hint of romance. Now she needed to flesh out her characters. The princess would be devoted to her father, the king, and would be properly maidenly, but with just enough spunk to make her interesting. Sandy then paused, trying to think of a worthy hero. He would be dashing and chivalrous, of course, and it went without saying that he was handsome. Probably blond and blue-eyed, she mused, since that was appropriate to the setting. He wasn't just a knight, but was an apprentice magician as well who had been drawn to the quest to rescue the princess by its unique danger. His bravery was without question, and he was willing to risk his life and limb for her, even though he had never really known her. All he knew of her was from a brief meeting in her father's great hall during a festival. Their eyes had met across the banquet table and he had been enraptured by her beauty. Now he couldn't rest while she was in danger from the wicked sorcerer.

Sandy sighed. They just didn't make them like that anymore. She knew that the true knight in shining armor she envisioned had never really existed like that in fact, but it would have been nice. Things would have been so much simpler if she just had to promise her hand in marriage to the man who risked his life to rescue her. That would eliminate wimps like Gregory. She smiled at that, saved her work, then shut down the computer for the night and went to sleep, looking forward to the day of sightseeing ahead of her.

The next day passed in a blur of cathedrals, monuments and museums. Sandy tried to drink everything in, but she was sure she would never be able to remember everything. It didn't help that she was foggy from lack of sleep or that her mind kept wandering back to her new story. That afternoon, when Rick finally called a halt to the tour and the group boarded the bus to go back to the hotel, she was about to collapse.

She fell into the front seat and started massaging her feet. When Rick got on he looked with amusement at her, but didn't say anything as he sat down.

"I hope you don't test us over what we were supposed to have learned today," she said wearily.

"Why? Too fast a pace for you?"

"Yes, that and information overload. And I didn't get much sleep last night."

"Didn't I warn you about that? I take it the writing went well."

"Very well. I can't believe I'm actually writing my own story."

"I hope you're not too tired to check out that little jazz club I told you about."

"Just let me rest a while and then I'll feel like celebrating."

He gave her an eager smile that was almost boyish, in great contrast to his usual too-charming-to-be-true smile. "Great. I know a wonderful place for dinner, then I'll show you Paris by night."

She was feeling too good about herself to have any doubts, so she chased the last warnings of caution from her mind and said, "Sounds wonderful." She was pleased at his delighted response and settled back into her seat to listen to his descriptions of everything they passed. The words didn't actually penetrate her brain, but his pleasure in sharing the city with her was almost tangible, and that gratified her.

When they got back to the hotel lobby she stopped him and asked if there was any word on her luggage yet. He asked at the concierge desk and brought back the news that they hadn't heard anything. Great, she thought, there goes my nap. The only good dress she had brought with her was in that bag, and that meant she had to do some quick shopping. With a promise to Rick to be ready by eight, she hurried to her room to clean up and change into something more befitting a Paris department store than her sweaty tourist clothes.

Back in the lobby, she asked the girl at the concierge desk where she could find a convenient place to buy something nice. The girl gave her directions, and Sandy thanked her with a smile. A large, chic department store was just around the corner, and once Sandy went inside and saw the glamorous selection of clothes, she had a sudden urge to splurge. Her mother had given her her credit cards, and she knew her mother would approve thoroughly of a Paris shopping spree, especially if she knew how quickly her daughter had gotten over her moping.

She found a flattering silk dress in a shade of teal that set off her golden brown hair and made her eyes look deep and rich. The dress was fairly low-cut, much more daring than anything she had ever worn before, and it skimmed her figure closely before swirling into a full skirt just below her hips. She bought strappy high-heeled sandals to match and on impulse bought a pair of delicate silk stockings. At the jewelry counter she picked out a pair of glittery golden earrings and a necklace. In the cosmetics department a salesgirl helped her choose a perfume that was feminine and exotic. Then she hurried back to the hotel with her purchases.

As she passed through the lobby she noticed the hotel's beauty salon. She stepped inside and asked if an appointment was necessary. The beautician didn't speak much English, and Sandy knew very little French, but between the two of them Sandy was able to get across that she would like to have her hair, nails and makeup done for a special evening. The stylist smiled broadly and gestured for her to set down her packages and hang the dress up. She peeked under the protective garment bag to check the color, then escorted Sandy over to the shampoo station and went to work.

An hour and a half later Sandy left the salon with her hair trimmed and curled into a more fashionable style, makeup that made her feel like a fashion model and finger and toenails painted a delicate shade of pink. When she got back to her room she couldn't help but stare at herself in the mirror. The sight was so unusual to her. Now she saw why her mother was always trying to get her to wear a little more makeup and to wear brighter colors.

She hadn't had time for a nap, and now she didn't want to risk messing up her hair in the couple of hours she had left before she was supposed to be ready, but the time in the beauty salon had relaxed her, so she spent the time working on her book. Thirty minutes before the time Rick was going to come pick her up she began to dress, eagerly anticipating his reaction.

At five minutes until eight Rick stood in front of the mirror in his room, straightening his tie. Three other ties lay discarded on the bed behind him. He frowned at his image in the mirror, not quite pleased, but he was out of ties. "Would you just calm down?" he scolded his reflection. "You're acting like a teenager on prom night. You're just taking the only woman travelling alone on your tour group out on the town so neither of you will be lonely. That's all." Still, in many ways he felt like a kid getting ready for his first date.

He checked his watch and hesitated over whether to arrive on time or to assume that she wouldn't be ready early and arrive late. Sandy didn't seem the type to keep anyone waiting. She was too conscientious for that. With one last glance in the mirror he left the room and went down the hall to Sandy's room. He rapped purposefully on the door, and she opened it almost immediately. He wasn't prepared for the sight that greeted him.

"Wow!" he said softly, then was stunned speechless. That silky, golden brown hair of hers curled gently around her shoulders. Her dress whispered slightly as she moved, and it showed off her slender figure to perfection. For the first time since he met her he noticed that she was wearing makeup, but it served only to make her eyes seem brighter and her mouth seem fuller. But what stunned him most of all was that seeing her this way didn't change the way he felt about her. He had been intrigued by her when she was standing on the deck of the boat, dressed in slacks and a shirt, her hair blown wildly by the wind and her face flushed by the outdoor air. Now the most noticeable change was in her attitude. She felt good about herself, and that made her sparkle.

"You look spectacular tonight, Cassandra," he said finally. She tried to correct him on her name, but he said, "There's nothing plain and simple about you tonight, so I'm afraid we'll just have to stick with what your mother named you. She must be a wise woman. I'd like to meet her sometime."

"Just read one of her books," she said with a smile. Her cheeks were flushed with pleasure, something no cosmetic could duplicate. He offered her his arm and escorted her to the elevators.

It was an evening right out of Sandy's most romantic dreams. First they went to a very elegant restaurant where Rick ordered for the two of them in his fluent French. They talked casually about everything and nothing through the whole meal. Rick was at his most charming, his dry wit at full force. Sandy smiled and laughed until her face hurt.

She, too, was more relaxed than she had been in ages. Even her evenings out with Gregory when they were engaged hadn't been as comfortable. She figured the difference was there was no pressure on her to impress him. She was constantly aware of the fact that she would never see him again after the end of the next week. That made all the difference for her.

When they had finished the main course, Rick suggested they wait until they got to the little jazz cafe to have dessert and coffee. "That sounds wonderful," she told him with a smile. He smiled too, and hurried to settle the bill.

Once they were on the sidewalk outside the restaurant, he turned to Sandy and said, "It's really not far to that cafe, and it's a beautiful evening. Do you think you'd like to walk? I mean, in those shoes?"

Sandy barely noticed the high heels she was wearing. She felt as if she were floating at least a foot above the pavement. "Walking would be fine," she told him. She took the arm he offered her and the two of them began to stroll across the city. Other couples, also enjoying the fine weather, strolled past them and around them. Sandy smiled to herself. If only Gregory could see her now, strolling down the streets of Paris, the most romantic city in the world, on the arm of a handsome man. She had to fight to keep from laughing out loud at the thought of what his face would look like if he saw the two of them together. Gregory had been very possessive. She had once been flattered about that, but she now knew better.

Rick turned toward her, a puzzled look on his face. "What?" he asked about her barely contained laughter.

She kept forgetting how perceptive he was. She wondered once more if he could read her mind. "Oh, nothing," she said airily, hugging his arm closer to her. "I was just thinking about how much I was enjoying this."

His eyes lit up. "I'm glad. Thank you for agreeing to come along with me tonight. I would have hated to have to spend the whole evening alone in my hotel room."

"Don't tell me you don't have a girl in every city you visit," she said teasingly.

He shook his head, and his expression was serious. "No. I just have the people in the group. It's a lonely business. That's why I'm enjoying tonight so much. I think I needed a friend."

She squeezed his arm. "So did I. Thank you." More than you'll ever know, she thought, then when they paused before crossing the street she quickly stood on tiptoes and kissed him on the cheek. She smiled inwardly as she noticed the flush rise up his face. He didn't reply, just urged her to cross the street when the way was clear.

The cafe was in the Montmartre district, which meant a steep climb up the hill. Sandy was out of breath by the time they got there, and she was beginning to be aware once more that her feet were hitting the pavement. Rick noticed her difficulty and slowed his pace, but he didn't seem to be affected in the least.

It was just barely dusk when they reached the cafe, and Rick suggested they have dessert sitting at one of the tables on the sidewalk. "The music won't heat up until later,'' he said. He ordered espresso and dessert for the two of them, and Sandy eased wearily back into her chair, grateful to be off her feet.

The district was beginning to come to life. She could hear music coming from other clubs and cafes, and brightly lit marquees gave the street a festive look. Looming over the whole scene was the white, onion-shaped dome of the Basilica of the Sacre Coeur, glowing softly in the pale moonlight.

Rick was silent for a while, seemingly taking in the sights himself, as if he'd never seen them before. She studied his face across the table. He really was handsome, she thought, and he was fun to be with. She wished she had met him in another time and place, when she was ready for a relationship and he wasn't running from commitment. If only they had met at a church function in Dallas, for instance. Then they could really have had something.

Suddenly she wanted desperately for him to say something sarcastic and witty so she could relax again. She needed that sardonic smirk and raised eyebrow to mar his classic features so she could stop thinking about him the way she had been.

She jumped when he did speak, and she wondered again if he could read her mind. ''I hope I didn't wear you out too much with that walk. I intend to do some dancing tonight now that I've gotten back into practice.'' He grinned and quirked that eyebrow at her, and she was able once again to relax in his company.

The waiter brought their dessert and coffee, and they

took their time enjoying it, chatting amiably about the trip thus far, their families and life in general. Sandy was feeling as if she'd known him forever by the time they finished eating.

The sounds of a jazz band warming up drowned out the last of their conversation, and Rick led her inside the cafe. A trumpet player, saxophone player, string bass and drum set were crowded onto the tiny stage. On the floor beside the stage was a battered old upright piano. The cafe was just starting to fill up with a mix of couples. Some, like Rick and Sandy, were dressed up, the men in suit and tie and the women in fancy dresses. Others looked more bohemian, dressed all in black with men and women wearing multiple earrings. There was an air of gentle seediness about the place that Sandy found exhilarating. She would never have gone into a place like this in Dallas.

Before she had a chance to object, Rick swung her out onto the dance floor. This cafe was more crowded than the hotel nightclub had been the night before, so he had to hold her closer. Their bodies were like one as they circled the dance floor. Sandy felt suspended in a bubble alone with Rick. The other couples were just a blur and the music seemed to echo in the distance. They didn't speak much as they danced; the music was too loud for that. Instead they concentrated on the dance.

It was early in the morning before the band quit playing. Sandy and Rick stumbled wearily out of the club, leaning on each other for support. "I think we should have sat out a dance or two,'' Rick gasped with a grin.

''There was a place to sit down?'' she asked, equally breathless.

''I don't know, but I don't think it was smart to dance every dance for four hours straight.''

''But it was fun,'' she pointed out.

He turned to her, settling his arm more comfortably around her waist. ''That it was.''

They walked on down the street in silence, too tired to make conversation. After several minutes he came to a stop under a streetlamp near a taxi stand. ''I don't know about you, but I'm beat, and I'm not looking forward to that long walk back to the hotel. What do you say we try to get a cab?''

She glanced up and down the street, but didn't see a taxi. Visions of the reckless, darting cabs she had seen earlier in the day went through her head, and she wondered if it would be so bad if they couldn't find one. ''I don't know,'' she said. ''Do you think we can get one this time of night?''

''Don't worry, one will come by eventually.'' He must have noticed her reluctance, for he chuckled and said, ''Parisian cab drivers aren't that dangerous, and you need to have the experience of at least one cab ride while you're in Paris.''

She shivered slightly at the thought of careening down those streets in a taxi. He frowned when he saw that, and asked, ''Are you cold?''

She nodded, noticing for the first time the cool breeze

that was sweeping down the street. He rubbed his hands up and down her bare arms. "I'm sorry about that. I forgot that I'm wearing this coat and a long-sleeved shirt while you're just in that dress." He shrugged off his jacket. "Here, take my coat." He draped it carefully around her shoulders, bending to pull the collar closed in front of her neck.

"Is that better?" he asked, his voice a husky whisper. She nodded silently, unable to break her gaze away from his eyes, which were only inches away from her face. She didn't know how long they stood like that, and she was scarcely aware of what was happening when he bent further and kissed her gently on the lips. It was a soft, warm kiss, and she found herself responding eagerly. His arms went around her and pulled her closer to him. His lips left her mouth to brush lightly across her cheek, and he buried his face in her hair. "Cassandra," he breathed.

That brought Sandy back to her senses. She pushed away from him with her palms against his chest and stared at the ground, unable to meet his gaze. The warning signals had gone off again in her brain, this time too strong to ignore. She was dangerously close to allowing herself to become emotionally involved with this man, and she was afraid to face the kind of hurt that could bring.

If he had responded to her pulling away with his usual charming smile or his sardonic raised eyebrow, if he had made a casual joke about the weather or the city, she might have been able to rid herself of her feelings for him then and there. But he didn't. He simply squeezed her two hands between his own and whispered, "I'm sorry. I shouldn't have done that." His voice and his eyes held that same gentle expression they had that evening above the Moselle river, when he had offered to listen if she needed to talk and she had almost wanted to throw herself into his comforting embrace. She couldn't resist that gentle side of him again.

She pulled her hands from his, linked her fingers around the back of his neck and, pulling him towards her, kissed him with a fervor she wasn't aware she was capable of. He was too stunned to react for a moment, then he wrapped his arms around her again, pulling her so close she could feel the pounding of his heart. While one arm held her firmly around the waist, he moved the other slowly up her back and began to run his fingers through her hair.

She had no idea how long they stood locked in each other's embrace. She was lost in the warmth of his gentle kisses, feeling safe in his strong embrace. Finally the kiss ended, but they still stood in each other's arms. She rested her cheek against his chest and he bent to kiss the top of her head.

Abruptly, he looked up, then waved an arm above his head. "Do you still want that taxi?" he asked. She nodded, afraid to trust her voice to speak and afraid her legs wouldn't hold steady enough to carry her back to the hotel. A cab screeched up to them and Rick helped her into the backseat as he told the driver their destination. They were barely settled in, Rick with his arm around Sandy and her head resting on his shoulder, when the cab lurched off down the street.

Sandy was too preoccupied to notice the harrowing ride through the dark streets. She was torn with conflicting emotions. She never wanted to leave the security of Rick's arms and she longed for his kiss, but she knew there was danger there. Could she survive another broken heart? He reached over and stroked her cheek, then tilted her chin up and kissed her again. Her doubts scattered and she lost herself once again in his embrace.

Neither of them was aware that the cab had come screeching to a halt outside their hotel until the driver cleared his throat noisily. Grinning sheepishly, Rick paid the driver then helped Sandy out of the cab. He led her into the hotel lobby with an arm around her waist. They didn't speak while they waited for the elevator or during the ride. He escorted her to her room, then gave her a lingering good-night kiss.

"Feel free to sleep in," he said at last, a semblance of his usual charming smile crossing his face. "There's nothing on the agenda for tomorrow morning."

She simply nodded, afraid to speak, and handed him his suit coat. He threw it jauntily across one shoulder and headed down the hall to his room as she unlocked her door. Fortunately, she was too exhausted to think much, and as soon as she had hung her dress, washed her face and brushed her teeth, she fell in bed and was asleep before her head touched the pillow.

Chapter Six

A bright beam of sunlight streaming through a chink in the curtain woke Sandy the next morning. She groaned and tried to cover her eyes, but she couldn't go back to sleep. Rolling over and picking up her watch to glance at the time, she groaned again when she saw how late it was. She had slept half the morning away, but she wasn't ready to get up just yet. She lay back on the pillow and stared up at the ceiling, letting her mind wander over the night before. Images of dinner, conversation and dancing drifted through her mind, along with the vivid sensations of the kisses that had followed. For a moment she wasn't sure how much had been real and how much had been a dream. There was certainly a dreamlike quality to it all, but the more she remembered, the more she knew it was real, even if her dreams had replayed the evening throughout the night.

She gave a deep, contented sigh. She couldn't remember being this happy in a long time. It felt good to have finally come out of that blue mood she had been in for weeks. Until now, she hadn't been aware just how bad she had been, but the contrast was amazing. Fighting back the impulse to giggle like a schoolgirl who had just been kissed by the football captain, she bounced out of bed and headed for the bathroom.

She paused by the vanity mirror and glanced at herself. Looking back at her was a glowing, bright-eyed young woman whose tousled hair still bore the remnants of last night's curls. She winked at her image and blew herself a kiss. "Sandy, sweetheart, you're beautiful!" she laughed before she continued toward the shower.

She had finished her shower and was vigorously toweling her hair dry while humming a tune she had heard the night before when there was a knock at the door. Still drying her hair, she moved closer to the door and looked through the peephole. It was Rick. At the sight of him her pulse started racing and her legs felt a bit shaky. "Just a second," she called to him, hoping her voice was more steady than her body's reaction.

She certainly didn't want to face him in just a bathrobe, but she wasn't sure if it was him or herself she was afraid of. She quickly pulled on jeans and a loose shirt, then ran her fingers through her still-damp hair to give it a semblance of style before she opened the door to him.

He burst into the room with a large, tapestried suitcase. "Surprise! Guess what just showed up at the front desk!"

"My luggage! They found it."

"Apparently it had quite a trip. Halfway around the world and back, according to all those tags. You might want to look through it to make sure everything got here okay."

"Thanks for taking care of this for me," she said as she placed the suitcase on the bed and opened it. Momentarily forgetting his presence, she rifled through the contents. Everything seemed to still be in the same meticulous order in which she had packed. She turned toward him with a big smile to find him looking back at her with more than just delight at the finding of the lost luggage in his eyes.

Then it hit her, a cold, hard ball of fear in her stomach. Suddenly she wanted nothing more than to be anywhere but there, in that room with him. She couldn't have explained it; it was sheer panic. Her heart pounding so loudly she was sure it must be audible down the hall, she could only stare at him, dreading and fearing the look she saw in his eyes. At that moment she knew this was more than just a game of flirtatious fun with a man she would forget as soon as she went back home. The walls that had crumbled to let him get past her defenses came back up to their full strength.

"Sandy?" Rick prodded.

She tore her gaze away from his, no longer able to meet his eyes. "Huh?" she stammered.

"Your things, is everything there?"

"Oh, yeah. Everything's fine."

"Good. I'm glad to hear that." After a moment of uncomfortable silence, he spoke again. "Are you all right?" he asked, the concern evident in his voice.

That concern made Sandy want even more to get as far away from him as possible. It was happening all over again and she couldn't bear it. She had sworn she wouldn't make that mistake twice. Struggling to keep her voice light, she faced him squarely and said, "I'm fine. I just didn't get much sleep last night and I'm beginning to get hungry."

The corner of his mouth quirked into a rakish almost grin. "I didn't get much sleep either," he said. "I have eaten breakfast, but I'm afraid the hotel isn't serving breakfast anymore. I'd be glad to accompany you someplace else. I could recommend a few places."

That was the last thing Sandy wanted. "No, no thanks," she insisted. "I was planning to do some shopping, so I might as well eat while I'm out."

"Shopping sounds like a great idea. I could take you to some wonderful shops . . ."

Steeling her resolve, she cut him off. "Oh, I like you too much to put you through that," she said as airily as she could manage. "You don't know what kind of shopper I am. Even my mother, who considers shopping an art form, hates to shop with me. Besides, I don't even know what I'm looking for. I intend to just go through stores and see what strikes my fancy." She glanced at him out of the corner of her eye and busied herself once again with her suitcase. He didn't exactly look convinced by her reasoning, so she added,

"You'd probably be better off finding something more entertaining to do. And I think the rest of the group is going to start accusing me of monopolizing the guide if I don't let you go for a while."

He sighed, and his wounded look was almost enough to send Sandy running into his arms to beg his forgiveness. "You're probably right," he said. "I have some paperwork to take care of anyway." He stood up and said hopefully, "Maybe I'll see you at dinner."

"Maybe," she said cheerfully and forced herself to look him in the eye. It was an effort to maintain her smile when she saw the hurt look on his face. She never would have thought of him as vulnerable, but there for a moment she felt she could see straight through to his soul, and that soul was wounded.

Then the window shut and he was once again Rick Hoffman, the charming, handsome tour guide who looked at the world with a smile and a raised eyebrow and never let himself be affected by anything. The change was startling. "Well, I've got to go pretend to do my job. Remember, for some of us, this is the way we earn a living," he said as he moved toward the door. "Good luck in the shops, or should I be wishing the salesclerks luck if they're having to deal with you?" At the door he paused to look back at her. "I'll see you later," he said, then left.

When he had shut the door behind himself, Sandy sank down onto the bed, suddenly exhausted. The atmosphere in the room seemed drastically lighter now that he had left. "How did you get yourself into this?"

she groaned out loud. She should have known better, she told herself. Here she was, just getting over a soured relationship with one man when she let herself start falling for another. It had been only a few days ago when she was vowing to avoid getting involved with anyone. That little idea of hers to go along with Rick's flirtation so she could forget Gregory had been a big mistake, and she knew she was about to face the consequences for that mistake.

That thought caused a sinking feeling in her stomach, but she knew what she had to do. Despite his all-too-obvious slick charm, Rick was too nice a guy for her to use just to make her forget someone else, and she had to break it off with him before he got hurt. It wasn't fair to him to let him get involved with her when she wasn't planning to really involve herself with him. She just had to find a way to let him know without hurting him—or letting on to him that she had just been using him. A return to her prickly ways of a few days ago was out of the question. She didn't like the way she had been then, and at least Rick had gotten her out of that mood. Instead, she needed to give Rick exactly what he wanted, a happy, enjoyable Sandy, while keeping him at a distance.

So, now keeping a good mood was up to her. It really should have been that way all along. She should have learned by now she couldn't depend on other people to make her happy. That never had worked. But what could she do here without Rick?

Then an old axiom of her mother's crossed her mind:

"When the going gets tough, the tough go shopping!" Sandy smiled. Her story to Rick didn't have to be a convenient lie. She suddenly felt like buying something hot pink or bright blue, something that would shock anyone who knew her. Her mother would approve.

Sandy got up and began dressing for a day in Paris shops. As she went through her wardrobe looking for something to wear, she was appalled at how boring her clothes were. It was time to change that, she decided. They wouldn't recognize her back home.

She decided to start her shopping expedition at the department store she had visited the day before. She wasn't necessarily looking for the chicest designer fashions. She just wanted something new and different. Inside the store, her eyes at first went automatically to the same sort of simple, classic, practical—and boring—things she habitually wore. But she didn't want to stay with the same old things. Instead, she allowed the sales clerk to suggest items.

The first armload of clothes Sandy took to the fitting room filled her with doubts, but as soon as she put on the jewel-toned, flowing skirt and blouse, she saw in the mirror the self-confidence she had felt growing within. From that moment, Sandy was like a woman possessed. She made up for every shopping spree she had never been on, buying a whole new wardrobe in one afternoon. She reasoned she could always find someplace to donate her old things. With a giggle, she imagined her mother's reaction to this. Penelope had been trying to get her daughter to buy clothes for years and despaired of ever getting her to wear anything fashionable. She would probably leap with joy to see Sandy in something new.

Sandy returned from her shopping trip tired but happy. She still had an hour to go before dinner time, so she decided to take a shower and try one of her new outfits. With a hairbrush and her blow dryer, she managed to imitate some form of the style the girl in the salon had given her the day before. After a moment's indecision, she chose a matching skirt and blouse in a soft green color, then put on some makeup. Feeling like a new woman, she grabbed her purse and headed to the dining room.

She was a few minutes late, so several members of the group were already there and eating. Rick wasn't in sight, and she sighed in relief at that. There was an empty place at Justin's family's table, so she went over to them and asked if she could join them. They all introduced themselves and began a pleasant conversation about the trip and their hometowns. Sandy was beginning to relax and enjoy herself when, out of the corner of her eye, she saw Rick come in.

She was relieved to see that all traces of his hurt, vulnerable look were gone. He looked her way, caught her eye and gave her that old smile of his that spoke of nothing more than flirtatious attention. She found herself smiling in return. She was actually looking forward to a bit of repartee with him. As long as they could keep things on this level, she might enjoy herself.

Rick glanced around the room, then his gaze came

back to Sandy's table and he began to approach. There was one seat left, the one next to Sandy. "Good evening, folks," he said to the group, then asked, "Mind if I join you? Everyone else seems to have been served, and I hate watching others eat."

Justin's father said, "Please join us."

Rick sat down, then asked Sandy, "How was your shopping trip today? Judging from the way you look this evening, I guess it was a success."

Sandy glanced down at the table, blushing at the compliment. This was just like the day on the Rhine. She looked back up at him. "It was very successful. By the way, is there room for any more luggage under the bus, or will I have to sit on my things?"

He cocked his head in mock deliberation, a wicked smile tugging at the corners of his mouth. "No, I'm afraid there's no more room," he told her.

"Do you know of any charity that would like a nice supply of boring but practical clothes?" she asked.

"I'm sure I can find one." Rick then turned his attention to the rest of the table. "And are you enjoying your stay in Paris?" he asked the family.

Justin's mother, who had introduced herself as Melanie Jordan, smiled and shook her head. "We've seen some interesting things, but we really haven't had a chance to . . ." she trailed off with a glance at her children.

Sandy had a burst of inspiration. "Well, I think Melissa, Justin, Scott and I could find something to do this evening and maybe you two could go out on the town.''

The Jordans looked at each other, then Melanie said, ''Oh, you wouldn't mind, would you?''

''Not at all,'' Rick said before Sandy could respond. ''That is, if the kids agree.''

Melanie looked at her children. ''Hey gang, how would you like to spend the evening with Miss Harrison and Mr. Hoffman?''

Justin shrugged his shoulders and said, ''Okay.'' Five-year-old Melissa just smiled, and three-year-old Scott clapped his hands.

Their mother was obviously thrilled. ''Thank you. We really appreciate this.'' She elbowed her husband, who grunted something that might have been thanks. ''We won't be out too late.'' She handed Sandy their room key so she could get to the children's things. They left soon after that, eager to have some time away from their three kids.

Sandy could have killed Rick for jumping in like that, but she had to admit he probably would be better at dealing with the kids than she was. It could even be fun. And she didn't have to worry about anything happening between them with three children around. She still would have to let him know she didn't appreciate him interfering, just later and not in front of the children.

When they had all finished dinner, Rick said, ''How does some ice cream sound?''

"I don't know, how does ice cream sound?" Justin quipped.

"Wise guy. Anyway, how about going to the park and getting some ice cream? It's still daylight for a while now." The kids approved and Sandy never passed up sweets.

They all got up from the table, and Rick picked little Scott up and gave him a ride on his shoulders. Melissa shyly took Sandy's hand while Justin shoved his hands in his pockets and came along. Sandy wondered how he was surviving without his computer game for so long.

"Duck!" Rick warned Scott as they went through a doorway. It really wasn't low enough for any danger, but the little boy squealed in delight at the excitement of his ride. The whole group strolled down the sidewalk to the park, looking for all the world like a young family on an outing.

Rick had stopped at a sidewalk vendor's cart and was waiting for Justin, Melissa and Sandy to arrive. Rick's eyes met Sandy's for a second, then he gave her a smile and deposited Scott in her arms. Rick stepped up to the vendor and ordered ice cream in his fluent French, then distributed the cones. They all sat on a park bench and ate ice cream in silence as they watched toy boats sailing in the sunset-tinted water of a fountain.

"Red skies at night, sailor's delight," Sandy murmured softly.

"What was that?" Rick asked.

"Oh, just some little rhyme my mother used to say. 'Red skies at morning, sailor take warning. Red skies at night, sailor's delight.' My father was in the Navy and it was something he used to say to her."

"I guess he didn't make a career out of the Navy if you were able to live in one place most of your life. You were lucky."

"Actually, he died when I was just a baby."

"Oh, I'm sorry. I didn't have any idea . . ."

She gave him a smile. "You couldn't have known. It's okay. I couldn't really miss him if I didn't know him, now could I?" They sat in silence, watching Justin and Melissa running around the fountain now that they had finished their ice cream. Scott still snuggled between Sandy and Rick on the bench, smearing ice cream all over his face in his enjoyment.

For the first time since she had met Rick, Sandy felt at peace. She didn't even feel the need to come up with something witty and wonderful to say. It was nice having a friend, she decided.

When the sun had dipped almost completely beneath the horizon and the shadows had grown long, Rick began rounding up the kids to return to the hotel. Scott had fallen asleep snuggled up against Sandy, and she gathered him up in her arms to carry him. Back at the hotel, Rick took the Jordans' room key from Sandy. "You go ahead and take Scott up to your room. We'll get the stuff we need and join you in a minute."

She carried the sleeping child up to her room, fumbled with the key in the lock, left the door slightly ajar, then sat on her bed, still holding Scott. She glanced down at his angelic face. It was hard to believe this was the same child who could scream bloody murder for a couple of hundred miles. She was still smiling in wonder at him when Rick and the other two burst into the room.

Rick tossed her a little blanket and a stuffed animal. She put Scott down near the headboard, covered him with the blanket and left the stuffed animal within easy reaching distance in case he woke up. Justin was once again engrossed in his game and Melissa was playing with a doll as she sang softly to herself.

The children thus occupied, and Rick so much better with the children than she was, Sandy pulled out her laptop computer and asked Rick, ''Mind if I try to get some work done? I'm here if you need me, but from the looks of things, you don't need much help.''

''Go right ahead.''

She settled down in an armchair with her computer on her lap. Once she started writing, her surroundings faded and she was once more in the place of the lovely heroine, who had just been kidnapped by the evil sorcerer. Then the hero had learned of her peril and had decided to drop his magical studies to search for her.

She had just put together the elements for the quest when, true to their word, the Jordans came back fairly early to collect their children. Rick lingered after they left, and Sandy's nervousness about him returned, but all he did was raise an eyebrow at her before he said,

"What possessed you to volunteer to keep that bunch? Have you ever even babysat in your life?"

"Not exactly," she hedged. "I just felt sorry for them to be in Paris and have to be cooped up with three kids instead of enjoying the town. I figure they need all the time alone they can get."

"Thanks," he said softly.

She laughed. "What do you mean, thanks? You rescued me from certain death by babysitting. Not only did I survive, thanks to you, but I even managed to get some work done. Thank you."

"Don't mention it. I just like to have all my tourists alive at the end of the trip. But I am grateful to you for helping me out in keeping everyone happy. That first night I told you I didn't want you to ruin things for others by being moody, but now you've gone beyond that to taking action to help others. I'm glad to see that."

She blushed at his praise and tried to wave it off. "Oh, I was just hoping for my chance to steal Justin's batteries. And where did you learn to be so good with kids?"

"I have a very large extended family over here, and I make up for what time I don't get to spend with my immediate family by attending every family gathering I can here. I think all of my cousins have at least three kids."

"And you must be everyone's favorite cousin."

He smiled. "Something like that. Good night. I'll see you in the morning."

Sandy closed the door behind him with relief. He hadn't even made a move to linger for more than conversation. It looked like he had gotten the hint and was settling into this new phase in their relationship. What she had said to him the night before had been true, she did need a friend. Now if only she could continue to be near him without her heart beginning to pound or that funny quivery feeling in her legs, and if there wasn't the danger that she might fall completely for his easy charm and gentle concern.

The next morning she began packing as soon as she dressed, for they were leaving Paris right after breakfast. It didn't take her long to shove as much as she could of the new clothes and the old clothes she wished to keep into her suitcases. The most boring, worn items in the bunch, which she hoped never to wear again, she bundled up into a dirty clothes bag to carry to Rick. He had said he knew of a few refugee organizations who would be thrilled to have such a donation.

She gathered all her bags—her load now heavier by one bag—and stumbled to the elevator, where she gratefully dropped her load as soon as the elevator door opened and she could stagger inside. When she reached the ground level, she picked up her bags once more and lurched into the lobby.

In the lobby, Rick was busy being his usual charming, efficient self. As soon as he saw Sandy with her unwieldy load, he hurried to help her. "Why didn't you call for a bellboy?" he scolded.

"I didn't want to bother. I made it downstairs, didn't I?"

He regarded her with a quirked eyebrow and a slight grin. "Yes, you did, didn't you." He shook his head wearily, sighed and said, "Go on in and have breakfast. We'll leave as soon as everyone's finished eating. And let the waiters serve you. They prefer that you don't try to do things yourself."

Sandy tossed her head and gave him a smug smile, then headed into the dining room. The breakfast of croissants and marmalade was wonderful. She savored every bite, knowing that the next morning she would be back to hard rolls and marmalade. For now, she enjoyed eating something she could actually bite into without hurting herself. Too bad the things were too flaky to smuggle out to keep her through the rest of the trip.

When she had finished her coffee and was sure she had brushed all the crumbs from her mouth and clothes, she went back out to the lobby. Most of the group was assembled, and Rick had them start getting on board the bus.

He didn't even hint that Sandy sit with him, so she went back to her usual seat beside Justin. As the bus crossed the French countryside, Justin taught Sandy to play his game and soon they were engaged in heated space battles. Sandy glanced up once to see Rick's amused glance when he walked past on one of his regular trips up and down the bus aisle. She wrinkled her nose at him and continued playing.

By the time they reached Heidelberg, back in Germany, Sandy had actually managed to beat Justin a couple of times at the game. He insisted it was simply because he was tired and hungry. Sandy reflected that he might be right, because the bus hadn't stopped for lunch. It was only through the forethought of the Foresters that the children hadn't become completely fussy. They passed out rolls they had bought before boarding the bus, explaining that they had been on those tours often enough that they knew to come prepared.

Sandy hadn't really noticed being tired and hungry. She was enjoying herself too much. It felt good to have friends in the group, and she was glad to get to know the people who sat nearby. She felt like a different person than the one who had reluctantly boarded the plane in Dallas. She had to admit it, her mother had been right. The trip had been good for her. A small voice at the back of her mind whispered that it hadn't been just the trip itself that had been good for her, but she shoved it away and started another game against Justin.

Rick hadn't even noticed that the bus driver hadn't made the scheduled lunch stop. He was too busy thinking and watching Sandy. He was pretty proud of himself. He had accomplished his goal of getting her to open up and enjoy herself. The transformation was remarkable, but he wasn't really surprised. He had seen the potential in her eyes that were too ready to laugh when she was trying to frown. If only he could stop thinking about her so much now that she no longer needed his special attention.

When the bus came to a stop in the parking area of the big castle in Heidelberg, he stood and stretched, suddenly aware of where he was. He scolded the driver for not making the lunch stop, then told the group that there was a restaurant and a snack bar on the castle grounds. They would meet for a tour in an hour.

He really didn't feel like eating, so he just walked around the castle grounds, mentally rehearsing the tour. As he thought of the tale of how the family of electors who lived in the castle had been cursed through the centuries, of how the castle itself had been burned by French armies and destroyed by lightning, he imagined Sandy's reaction to the story. That was the sort of thing she would love. He could see the way her eyes would widen and the way a slow smile would spread across her face as she became lost in the story of the past.

He smiled as he thought of that and found himself looking forward to giving a tour for the first time in months. He realized that she wasn't the only one who had gained something from their friendship. She had given him something valuable, a new way of looking at life, a way of seeing the wonder in everything. Whether he liked it or not, she had affected him. He didn't allow that to happen very often. He glanced at his watch and returned to the motor coach.

Sandy was one of the first out of the snack bar. She licked her ice cream cone and strolled around the parking area, enjoying the summer sun. Out of the corner of her eye she caught a glance of someone walking up to the bus. From the glint of the sun on golden hair, she guessed it must be Rick. Despite—or perhaps because of—the ease she had felt with him last night, she was reluctant to approach him. But she was suddenly filled with such a bubbling mood that she had to share it with someone. Why not Rick?

Still licking her ice cream cone, she sauntered up to him and leaned against the bus. "Is the weather always this gorgeous here?" she asked as casually as possible while she fought to keep from bursting out laughing with the sheer delight of being alive in the sunshine and eating an ice cream cone.

He laughed slightly. "Actually, we've been quite lucky. I've known many a summer when it's cold and damp the whole time. I've had tours where we wore raincoats and carried umbrellas for two whole weeks."

"Well, I'm glad I came at the right time. This is much nicer than back home. It's just as sunny, and not as hot and miserable."

He smiled and shook his head. "I hope you haven't just jinxed us. Now we'll probably get the more typical German weather the rest of the trip. I'll be sure to let everyone else know whose fault it was."

"I'm not that powerful, am I? But just in case, I'll be sure to buy an umbrella at the gift shop here. That will prevent rain."

He frowned as if to consider the thought. "I don't

know if it would be such a bad thing if it did rain. I think you need to see Germany in its natural state.''

Sandy could hardly believe she was standing here talking about the weather. It was the most inane small talk she could think of, yet it was still all right with her.

He gave her a suspicious glance. ''Do you always get so excited about the weather?''

''What?''

''I don't think I've seen you with such a big smile before. I may have to go find my sunglasses.''

She laughed. ''Oh, I'm just in a great mood.''

''I can tell. What's so great?''

''Well, I have all my luggage, it's all full of new clothes, and I'm standing in the sunlight outside a magnificent castle as I eat an ice cream cone. All is right with the world.''

He grinned and shook his head. ''I'm glad to hear that. Now, who are you and what have you done with Sandy Harrison?''

She gave him a good-natured punch on the arm. ''It's all your fault, you know. If you'd just left me alone in my room I would have continued to be moody and sullen. Now that you've forced me to have fun, you have to deal with it.''

''Oh, such independence. I'm proud of you.''

She blushed a bit, suddenly aware that she was pushing just a little bit too far for her own comfort. It wouldn't do to give him the wrong idea again. She quickly changed the subject. "Do you do any tours of eastern Germany?" she asked.

He shrugged. "My company does some. I don't lead them, though. I never really spent much time there. This is the area I'm more familiar with, and there's more than enough in western Germany to keep us occupied for ten days. I have some brochures of our other tours in case you're interested in coming back some time and visiting the east. I have guides who are quite knowledgeable about the area."

By this time the other tourists had arrived and immediately expressed an interest in the brochures, preventing Sandy from asking him any more questions. When the whole group had gathered, Rick began to lead them around the grounds of the castle.

Instead of the usual mass of names and dates he told of a rich, exciting history of curses and destruction, love and war. Sandy found herself getting caught up in the story, carried away by his narrative. She glanced up at him and found herself looking him straight in the eye, as if he were speaking to her in particular. She felt as if this were a private conversation between them. The others in the group didn't seem to notice anything different; they just paid more attention to the guide's description than they usually did. Even Justin seemed captivated. That gave Sandy an idea.

Chapter Seven

As soon as they had finished the tour and were back on the bus, Sandy turned to Justin and asked, "Have you ever read anything about castles?"

He shrugged. "I don't read much."

"There are a lot of great stories out there just as interesting as the ones Rick told today."

"Yeah?"

"Yeah. What do you say we play a Nintendo tournament, best two out of three, and if I win, you read a book, like maybe *Robin Hood* or *Ivanhoe* or *The Black Arrow*."

"And if I win?"

She smiled smugly. "I don't intend to lose."

He snorted. "Yeah, right. What do I get if I win?"

"Let me think." She frowned for a while, racking her brain. She really didn't intend to lose, because winning meant that she might be free of the computer game's beeps for a while during this trip. "I'll buy you a box of German chocolates."

The boy nodded. "Cool. Okay, when do you want to play?"

"Now. We have some time before we get to the hotel."

"Deal. Let's go."

Sandy was still a novice, but she had figured out ways that the game seemed to work. She had always been good at analyzing things, and she had been practicing. She won the first game by a close margin.

"No fair!" Justin exclaimed. "That's just the first game."

"I used to be quite the pinball wizard when I was your age. That requires more stamina. And I spent my share of time with Space Invaders." They began to play again, but Sandy was distracted when Rick came up the aisle to see what the excitement was all about. The sight of him leaning over Justin's seat was enough to throw Sandy's concentration off. Justin won that game.

"Best two out of three," she reminded him.

"What's going on here?" Rick asked with a smile.

"Justin and I are having a tournament. If I win, he has to read a book."

Rick nodded and winked at Sandy. He knew what she was up to. "Good luck to the both of you." He headed back down the aisle to the front of the bus.

Sandy managed to win the last game by taking advantage of a moment of distraction when Justin saw a bright red sports car whiz by. We all have our weaknesses, she mused. Hers was blond tour guides, his was red sports cars. She tried to maintain her adult manners and not gloat too much about winning, and Justin didn't seem very upset. Maybe he had been interested in the history of the old castle and just needed an incentive to read.

"Okay, now you have to find me a book," he told her. "And it has to be in English."

"Don't worry, I'll find something." To be free of the computer game for a couple of days she would piece something together from memory if she had to.

Soon the bus stopped at an inn across the river from the castle. As Sandy got off the bus, Rick asked, "How did the tournament go?"

She gave him a smug grin. "Do you know where I could find an English-language edition of *Ivanhoe?*"

"There's a good bookstore not far from here. They keep a few English books around for the large American population here." He gave her directions.

"Thanks," she said as she turned to head to her room.

He stopped her just before she left. "Are you interested in seeing the fireworks tonight?" he asked.

"Fireworks?"

"Yes, every year they reenact the burning of the castle with fireworks. We got here at just the right time."

"Yes, I suppose I will watch. It would be a shame to pass up an opportunity like that. I might as well experience everything while I'm here."

A big smile broke out over his face. "Great. I know

just the place to watch them from. We'll have to get there early because it gets pretty crowded up there. I'll meet you at dusk in the lobby.''

Before she could respond, he was off, whistling softly to himself.

At dinner, she sat with the Jordan family and gave Justin the book she bought. He looked at the cover, then turned it over to look at the back. ''Thanks,'' he said. ''It looks pretty cool.''

That was high praise coming from Justin. ''You're welcome,'' she told him. Then she had another idea. ''Mr. Hoffman said there will be fireworks at the castle tonight. They reenact the burning of the castle. He said he knows of a great place for watching them. Want to join me?''

Justin pursed his lips in thought, then nodded. ''Sure. I could do that.''

''Wonderful. I'll see you at dusk. And I want to hear how the book's coming by then.''

He groaned and rolled his eyes, but he didn't look too unhappy. Sandy smiled with satisfaction. It was nice to be able to reach out to the boy. Maybe she could do for him what Rick had done for her.

Rick felt a pang of disappointment when he saw Sandy arrive with the kid, but he quickly shoved it aside. Justin needed some attention, and it was doing Sandy good to help him. Still, he wondered how much of it was Sandy wanting to help the boy, and how much was her fear of being alone with him. Something had scared her after that night in Paris, and as much as he was glad about their unspoken mutual agreement to keep things on a strictly friendly basis, he wondered what it was that had hurt her before. He was more sure now than ever that something must have happened to her to scare her away from closeness like that. Or, he reflected, she could be like he was, never having to make a commitment to anyone other than his family because he was always moving.

He gave Justin and Sandy a big smile. "Hi Justin. Glad you could join us. Are you enjoying your book?"

The boy rolled his eyes at Sandy. "Gee, Sandy, did you have to tell everyone?"

"There's nothing to be ashamed of. I told you I used to play pinball all the time, and this is easier. And it's perfectly all right to be caught reading."

"I guess the book is okay," Justin told Rick. "I'm almost at the part with the joust. You know, Sandy said if I liked the stories you told today about the castle then I might like the book."

Rick glanced up at Sandy, who was blushing slightly and leaning forward so that her hair covered her face to hide it. "I'm glad you liked my stories," he told the boy, but the intent of the statement was aimed at Sandy.

"They were okay. Did the castle really get struck by lightning just when they finished fixing it up? I guess it really was cursed."

"Maybe." Rick led them up a path that led from

behind the inn up the side of the hill opposite the castle, overlooking the river. A large crowd had already gathered to watch the fireworks. Rick wove his way through the crowd to a clear spot almost on the edge of the hill. Sandy flinched back from the steep incline, but Rick put an arm around her waist to steady her. "It's okay, you won't fall," he murmured in her ear.

She turned toward him, her face half stricken with fear, but her eyes were soft and pleading. Emotions seemed to do battle across her delicate features, but she didn't say anything. She didn't shove him away either, and he was unaccountably thrilled by that small concession.

While they waited for the fireworks to start, Rick told them about the river and the beautiful old bridge that spanned it. "It's said to be a very romantic bridge," he said, then watched for Sandy's reaction. She blushed, and he felt as if he could sense the heat from her cheeks.

It wasn't long before the first of the fireworks began. At the first loud bang Sandy jumped and edged closer to Rick. He tightened his hold on her, and she didn't try to move away, even after she relaxed and became accustomed to the loud noises. He bent over so that her hair blew in his face and he could smell her perfume. The sensation of being so close to her, feeling her pressed up against him, smelling her sweet scent, was intoxicating. He barely noticed the fireworks above the castle because of the fireworks going off in his brain.

The awareness of those feelings was like a rocket

going off within him. He had always been afraid of permanence, of commitment. He had learned at an early age that allowing himself to become close to someone other than his family always meant that he would get hurt. And there was the seductive knowledge that no mistake was permanent. He knew that in a couple of years he could start over again with a clean slate. That wasn't an upbringing that led to long-term relationships. It was always a relief to say goodbye and begin again. But here he was in what had to be the most temporary of relationships and he suddenly didn't want to let go of this woman who had taught him to see the romance in what to him was familiar. He had reached out to her pain, and in doing so had invested a part of himself he could never get back.

"I love you, Sandy Harrison," his mind screamed with the ecstasy of revelation, but he bit his lip and forced himself to stay silent. Now wasn't the time to force the issue. He still had several days, plenty of time in which to be sure of his feelings and hers, but if he hadn't managed to win her over by then, he swore to himself that he would tell her, no matter what. He couldn't let her go after she had changed his way of looking at life.

The fireworks came to a spectacular finish, but Rick barely noticed until Sandy relaxed and edged away from him. He loosened his hold on her reluctantly. The three of them began to make their way back down the path, the boy running ahead and Rick and Sandy picking their way more carefully behind him. Once Sandy stumbled and grabbed for Rick's sleeve. He caught her and held on to her elbow for the rest of the trip, relishing the chance to touch her again. It was a chance he knew he wouldn't have the next day in the daylight.

When they reached the inn, she disengaged herself from his hold, said a cheery goodnight and took Justin off to his parents' room. Rick watched her go, remembering the feel of her in his arms. He felt so empty and cold now that she was away from him.

So, this was what it was like to fall in love, he thought. After all these years of avoiding anything that stirred such deep feelings, it had snuck up on him and caught him unawares as soon as he let his guard down. Why now? he silently asked the stars above. He didn't know what to do, whether to let her know and try to win her love in return in the days they had left together or to just let her go and hope that fate brought them together again.

He didn't like this empty, cold feeling he now had without her, and he couldn't face the rest of his life feeling like that. That left only one option, and he still didn't know exactly what to do about it, but he had no choice. He couldn't let her go now that he had found her. He took one last deep breath of cool night air which was still scented with the remains of the fireworks, then went into the inn for what he had a feeling would be a restless night.

Sandy knew she had to get some writing done, despite the fact that she couldn't focus her thoughts.

Everywhere she went she got new ideas for her book and they were coming too quickly for her to arrange them all. She eased back against the pillows on her bed, her laptop computer settled on her knees, and began to think. She liked the idea of the burning castle. Maybe the sorcerer would set his castle on fire in hopes of trapping the hero. The hero would fight his way through the flames to get to the heroine before the villain could spirit her away. The hero would put his strong arms around her and keep her safe from her fears as they watched their enemy go up in flames, or so they thought.

That was good. It was so real she could almost feel it. Then it hit her. She had felt it, that very night, when Rick had held her close when she was startled at the noise. It was purely a physical reaction, she told herself. It was human nature to seek warmth and security, especially in times of fear. Any man could have had that effect on her.

She shrugged off the thoughts and sensations and returned to her writing, but that was disturbed when she realized her mental image of the hero had taken on Rick's face. Why was this man being etched into her brain? Well, she reasoned, he was handsome, and he was around all the time. That was it. He did make a splendid hero, with a few artistic changes. Her hero wouldn't be a casual flirt. He would want a committed relationship. He'd marry his land together with the heroine's and together they'd grow strong. Somehow she couldn't picture Rick owning land. He didn't seem the sort to be able to stay in one place for very long.

Only a few more days and she wouldn't have to see him again. Then she could concentrate. Not that she wasn't enjoying herself. She was, and her mother had been right. The trip had been good for her. She had come out of her moody depression, her spirit had awakened and she was on her way to finding out just who Cassandra Harrison really was, independent of her mother, Gregory or any man.

The next day's drive was pure bliss for Sandy. It didn't matter that the normal gray, damp German weather Rick had told her about had come back. Justin was engrossed in his book, and never once brought out his computer game. Sandy passed the time gazing out the bus window at the misty scenery as they travelled south from Heidelberg to the Black Forest. The very name of the forest conjured up vivid images for Sandy. She knew her fertile imagination was more than likely wrong, but still she had always thought of the Black Forest as some mysterious, magical place. She was looking forward to arriving there.

It wasn't long before Rick's voice coming over the speaker interrupted her thoughts. ''We are approaching the famous spa and casino city of Baden Baden,'' he said. ''This is on the northern edge of the Black Forest. We will stop here for a couple of hours, then travel on to Freiburg, which is where we will stay for the night.''

Rick stopped Sandy as she got off the bus. "Planning to hit the casinos?" he asked with a grin.

She shook her head firmly. "No. I'm not the gambling type."

"I didn't think so."

"What do you mean by that?" she asked, her defensive stance belied by the smile she couldn't suppress.

"Nothing. You're just not too big on risks, are you?"

"And what's wrong with that? It keeps me out of trouble."

"But trouble can be a lot of fun," he told her with a wicked grin lighting his blue eyes. "What I was trying to ask was, what are you planning to do while we're here?"

"There's no tour planned?"

"There's not much to walk past and talk about. I prefer to let people find their own things when we're going to be here for such a short time. This is mainly for leg-stretching purposes. I would be glad to show you around, if you like."

"Hmm," she pondered. "It looks like I could be on my own in a strange city. Who knows what kind of trouble I could get into." She winked at him, then frowned again. "Or, I could get the deluxe guided tour. Then, of course, I could still get into trouble with you around. Oh, well, I guess I'll go with you."

"Not if you don't want to."

"Really, I want to," she insisted. "Lead on, guide."

He took her by the arm and obliged. He showed her the gothic cathedral, some winding cobblestone streets and the park where old men played a game of chess on a huge outdoor board with chess pieces almost as big as themselves. Just like that last evening in Paris, Sandy felt completely at peace in his company. The easy camaraderie of friendship made even the gray day seem bright.

They strolled through the park, arm in arm, talking and laughing. Rick was telling stories of some of his experiences leading tours. "How did you get started in this business, anyway?" Sandy asked after they had both recovered from laughing at one story.

"I fell into it. I was wandering around Europe, trying to live off my wits and living off my relatives when that failed. Once, I came across a huge tour group that the guide couldn't handle. He had gotten lost and asked me for directions in terrible German. He was relieved to find that I was American and also could speak the native language. He hired me on the spot to help them find their motor coach again and show them the sights along the way."

"So, you went to work for him?"

He snorted. "Not likely. I wouldn't want to work for a shady outfit like that. But he did spread my name around, and most of the tour companies knew that if they needed an extra guide who knew Americans and knew the country and the language like a native, I was there. I ended up getting hired by one of the big companies that does package tours.''

''That was quite a move up in the world. You went from being a bum to owning your own company. When did you decide to go off on your own?''

''That was just a few years ago. I contracted out with an airline to do a package tour, and I leased a bus and led it myself. Now we own the motor coaches and I have several guides with their own areas of expertise. The next step for us is to be based stateside, so we can market ourselves better.'' Resignation tinged his voice on the last sentence.

''You don't sound like you look forward to it.''

He sighed. ''I have mixed feelings. I miss my parents and my brother, and I miss our home. I'm also ready to settle down. After a few years of this the wanderlust has died down a bit. Still, I will miss it.''

''When are you going to move?''

''I'm not sure, but something tells me it may be pretty soon.''

''Why's that?''

''Oh, just a feeling I have.'' He held her arm tighter but didn't meet her eyes.

They walked in silence for a minute, until Sandy asked, ''How many tourists have you had like me?''

''Like you? In what way do you mean?''

''You know, standoffish, not wanting to get involved. Someone who actually made you work to be charming.''

He laughed. ''I think you're the worst I've seen in

a long time. Of course, there was that lady who had bought the tickets with her husband, but he died before the trip. I offered to refund them, but she insisted she wanted to go and brought along her sister. Now, they were miserable, because they didn't get along at all, yet they were stuck sharing a room for two weeks. I'm amazed they both lived through the trip. I thought they'd kill each other.''

"Was I as bad as that?"

"Worse. They had each other. I got the feeling they were happy when they were fighting, and being angry with her sister helped the one lady get over the loss of her husband. Now, you were a unique case. Not many people come to Europe alone when they're in a bad mood.''

"I didn't want to go, but my mother surprised me with the trip.''

He looked at her intently. "Are you still upset you had to come?''

She shook her head. "No, she was right. It was good for me. I needed a change of scenery so I could forget . . .'' her voice trailed off.

"Forget what?'' he asked gently.

"I forgot!'' She laughed at her own joke, then continued, "Getting away was good, too, because I sort of found myself once I got away from the everyday things. I know that sounds kind of dumb, but I think it really is true.''

"It doesn't sound dumb. You really have become more at ease with yourself. I've seen a change.''

Sandy didn't respond. She just continued to walk, enjoying the warmth of him next to her on the damp, cool day. She had needed a friend, and that's what he was, she realized. He was someone she could count on to cheer her up, to make her laugh, and to listen when she needed to talk. Friends like that, other than her mother, had been few. She never had been good at opening up to people. Now here this man was who was so winning and caring that she had come out of her shell. Impulsively she stopped, stood on her tiptoes and kissed his cheek.

"What was that for?" he asked, visibly stunned.

She blushed. "Oh, just thanks for being so nice. You didn't have to be, and it was a big help." More than you'll ever know, she concluded to herself.

"Glad to help. Anytime you need me, I'll be there." He sounded like he truly meant it and wasn't just giving her a line. He looked away from her, watching the old men continue their game. "You've helped me, too."

"I have?" she asked, puzzled.

"Yes. With your silly romantic stories you made me look at things again. Can you believe I had actually been getting bored? Now I'll never be able to look at a castle again without thinking about your stories about the princesses and the knights." He bent and gave her a quick kiss on the cheek, murmuring as he did so, "Thanks."

Her cheek tingled from the kiss. It had sent unexpected sensations through her, sensations too strong to have come from a simple peck on the cheek. Her heart began to pound. So much emotion had been conveyed through that gentle brushing of her cheek with his lips. Neither of them spoke until they reached the bus. There Rick stopped her and said, "Would you like to sit up front with me?"

She considered for a second, then said, "Only if you'll tell me something about the Black Forest."

He smiled. "Agreed. I suppose you've already got a vivid mental picture of what the Black Forest is."

"You know me too well," she said ruefully. He laughed and escorted her onto the bus. She went to get her totebag from the back of the bus and brought it up to her seat next to Rick.

"I take it your ploy worked," he said as she sat down and the bus started moving.

"Huh?"

"You got that kid to quit playing the game and actually read a book."

She sighed. "Yes, that is better, but he still doesn't even look out the window. I'm afraid the whole trip has been wasted on him."

"I wouldn't say so. You may have gotten him excited about reading. That's worthwhile."

"But he still won't have anything to remember from the trip."

"You'd be surprised. And the best castles are to come. There's one that will astonish even you. By the time he's finished Ivanhoe he'll be excited about it." He reached over and patted her hand. "You've paid more attention to him than his parents have on this trip. They probably used that game as a babysitter and you've shown him something different.''

''How do you always know the right thing to say?'' she asked with a faint smile.

''Just one of my many skills.''

She raised an eyebrow. ''Oh.'' They rode without speaking for several minutes before Sandy said, ''Well, Mr. Tour Guide, where's this Black Forest?''

''You're in it.''

''What?''

''See the trees?''

''But they're just ordinary firs.''

''Yes, but there are millions of them and they're very dense.''

She sighed deeply. ''I've got to stop getting my hopes up.''

''Don't do that. Keep having your hopes high. You deserve it.''

She looked him quizzically. ''What does that have to do with romanticizing the name of a forest?''

''It has a lot to do with everything. Don't ever give up your dreams. I like the way you look at the world.''

She was beginning to wish she'd sat in the back again, but, she reasoned, she couldn't run from a man just because he caused strong feelings in her. She could handle a man who thrilled her with his presence and made her melt with his words. She gazed at him for a moment, then said with an ironic smile, ''Now, that sounds like a different person than the one who met us at the airport. As I recall, you made fun of me for my romantic notions.''

''That was back in my cynical days. It's so much more fun to have romantic notions. Next thing you know, I'll be reading your books.''

''If I ever finish one.''

''How is it going?''

She shrugged. ''Well enough. I've got a good portion of an outline done, and I think I'm doing pretty well. Now I just need some good writing time.''

''And that's a cue for me to leave you alone this evening once we're at the hotel.''

''Well, since it doesn't look as if any witches or gnomes are going to come out of the so-called Black Forest to spirit me away, it looks like I do need to work. When I get home I'll just have tons of my mother's tapes to transcribe.''

He looked out the window for a while, then said, ''If you were in the middle of that forest you'd think it was black enough. It's so dense light doesn't penetrate well to the forest floor. We're just in a clearing made for the highway. And this is the land of the woodsmen and woodcarvers. I'm afraid gnomes don't exist anymore, though.''

''I know,'' she sighed. ''And neither do witches or enchanted princesses or knights in shining armor or anything like that.''

''You'd be surprised. They probably do exist, but you just wouldn't recognize them. They have to change to fit the times, just like everything else.''

"Well, let me know when you see one. I'd like to know what they're up to now."

"I'll be sure to let you know the moment I see any of your mythical creatures."

"Good, you do that." And with that she turned back to the window, just on the off chance that she could spot something unique and magical.

Rick, showing his usual perception, did leave her alone that evening. As she sat struggling for words, she wanted desperately to talk to him again. He was so easy to talk to, and she felt he might be able to help her sort through her confused feelings. The problem was, he confused her even more.

By the next morning she had forced her feelings into a kind of equilibrium and she was ready to face the day. They left the Black Forest by mid-morning and headed toward the Bavarian Alps. Sandy continued to sit with Rick, enjoying his company and his amusing stories. The trip passed quickly, and Sandy scarcely noticed the spectacular scenery as they passed Lake Constance and entered the steep mountains.

After a quiet lunch at a small town along the way, Sandy asked, "When do we get to see that fabulous castle you were telling me about, the one you said would make even Justin take notice?"

"This afternoon."

"It better be good. I'm trying not to imagine it, but I'm sure my romantic imagination will top reality as usual."

"Not even your imagination can top Ludwig's."

"Who's Ludwig?"

"The mad, castle-building king of Bavaria."

"Okay, so now I'm mad?"

"I didn't say you were. He was."

"Oh. So how far away is this castle?"

"About an hour away."

"I'm looking forward to it."

Rick hardly knew what to think about Sandy's behavior toward him. For the most part she was warm and friendly, and seemed to truly enjoy his company. Yet she still kept a subtle emotional and physical distance between them. He didn't know what to do. Every moment he spent with her was both pleasure and pain. He wanted so much to express his feelings for her. Keeping them bottled up was torture. But he risked losing everything if he acted rashly.

For now he was enjoying her easygoing friendship. Friendship could lead to so many other things, but he wished he had more than a few days. She was relaxing some, and he hoped that by the time the tour was over with she might relax enough for him to be able to look her up when he got back to the states. Dallas had a big airport, and that might work as a stateside headquarters for his company.

He was anticipating the arrival at Neuschwanstein almost as much as Sandy was. Even at his most jaded, the spectacular, fairy-tale castle never ceased to awe him. He could hardly wait to see Sandy's reaction. As the bus rounded a bend in the road and reached the peak of a hill, the castle suddenly came into view, its turrets framed by the mountains behind it. Rick watched Sandy's face carefully as she first saw the castle.

Her eyes widened and her jaw dropped open. "Oh, my," she gasped. "Now that's what I call a castle."

"Neuschwanstein," he told her, "Mad Ludwig's dream castle."

"I think Sleeping Beauty must have lived there."

"It really isn't that old, not much more than a hundred years. Poor Ludwig was a bit behind his time. I think he wished he had been a medieval king." He grinned at her. "You and he would have agreed on a lot of things. For one thing, you both have the same idea of what a castle should be, and you're not afraid to romanticize."

She turned to him. "What's it like inside?"

"Pretty impressive. Ludwig may have liked the old-fashioned look, but he also liked modern conveniences. There's central heat and a sort of telephone system. The throne room was never finished, though."

"That's all right. You were right, this is a spectacular castle."

"Glad to have pleased you." He felt a bit of satisfaction. Finally he had managed not to disappoint her. This had to be the most romantic setting for someone like her, and he could play Prince Charming as well as anybody.

When the tour bus came to a stop after a steep climb

up to the castle, Rick extended a hand to help Sandy off the bus. "My lady," he said gallantly. She wanted a knight in shining armor, she would get him, he vowed.

Chapter Eight

Sandy was truly awestruck at this castle. She hardly heard anything Rick said, she was so busy daydreaming about knights and ladies, of pageantry and pomp. She knew he had said the castle really wasn't that old, but it still looked like the kind of place she had imagined in countless fairy tales. She felt that if she went into the turret of the highest tower she would find Sleeping Beauty there. For once, she didn't try to restrain her overactive imagination; she relished the lush details it conjured up. So what if she was being silly, she was enjoying herself thoroughly and there was plenty of time to be in touch with reality later on.

In her flights of fancy Rick suddenly appeared as her knight errant, and she didn't even try to shake the image from her brain. With his Teutonic good looks and his continental manners he was tailor-made for the role. What maiden wouldn't want a protector who could make her laugh, but who also could be warm and gentle?

She drank in the details of the castle: the great empty

throne room, still unfinished after all these years, with no throne to seat the long-dead monarch, the swans that were repeated throughout as a motif in the decor, the swan-shaped door handles, the figurines, the frescoes. It was all too beautiful to be real.

Rick's voice behind her didn't bring her too far into the present. "Sandy," he said softly, "we've finished the tour. You're free to walk around outside for a bit and stretch your legs."

"Oh, yes, thank you," she murmured dreamily, noticing that they were back outside in the courtyard.

He gave her a knowing smile. "Let me guess, you're off in one of your imaginary worlds."

She nodded, but didn't say anything.

"Share it with me. What do you see?"

She could feel the blush mounting in her cheeks. She could hardly tell him he was the hero of her fantasies. That would give him the wrong idea. "I know you told me this castle was really fairly new, but I was imagining the court, with all the knights and ladies, and of course, Sleeping Beauty in the tallest tower."

He leaned his head back and looked up at the tower. "You're right," he said after a while, "That does look like a good place for Sleeping Beauty."

She laughed nervously. "I know I do sound ridiculous, but I've picked up material here for a dozen books."

"The trip's been worthwhile for you, then?"

"Yes, very much so. I'll have to thank my mother. But, she'll never let me forget she was right."

"That's what mothers are for. Now, do you want to walk around a bit?"

She nodded, and he placed a hand at the back of her waist to guide her as they walked to the edge of the courtyard. The view of the mountains was stunning. Their majesty made Sandy feel small and weak in comparison, and she leaned a bit closer to Rick to draw from his strength. He responded by adjusting his hold on her so that his arm encircled her waist. She rested her head against his shoulder and gazed at the scene in silence. Finally she said, "This has been one of the best times in my life."

"What? This here today?"

"No, the whole trip. It sounds overdramatic, but I think I'm going to go home a different person than I was when I left."

"I don't think you're a different person. You're just letting yourself be the person you really are."

She pulled away from him enough to look at him. "I don't understand."

"You were busy running from something—I'm not sure what, someone else, maybe—but you were also hiding from yourself. I think you've just realized who you are away from your familiar settings and you've decided you like that."

She leaned up against him again and thought about what he had said. Her mind was reeling. He knew her so well, had seen things in her no other person ever had. Why did a man like this have to come into her life at this time, when she needed to be her own person, when she was still afraid of being hurt, when she would only know him for a short while before losing him? "If only we had more time," she said softly, hardly aware she had spoken aloud.

It was his reaction that told her she had voiced her thought. He stiffened as a tremor ran through his body, then he pulled her even closer, wrapping both arms around her and holding her tight, as if he would never let her go. He didn't speak except to whisper her name. She slipped her arms around his waist and held him, too. His arms around her almost crushed the breath out of her, but she didn't care. She only wanted to be held tighter and forever, but she knew that couldn't be.

Finally he released her and stepped back, then reached out and brushed a tear off her cheek with his thumb. Not aware that she had been crying, she rubbed angrily at her eyes. Neither of them spoke for a while. They just stared into each other's eyes, not wanting to break the moment. She was the first to speak. "They're going to wonder if we fell into that gorge," she said, her voice sounding shaky to her own ears.

He nodded. "You're right. We don't want to panic the troops." He took her hand and led her back to the bus. While he waited outside for the group to gather, she got on and attempted to repair her makeup. She didn't know what had possessed her to cry at a time like that, but she did know she could no longer deny what she felt for him. Of all the luck, she thought. She would have to find the man of her dreams only to lose him after ten days. But she could enjoy the time she had with him, and return home that much more fulfilled. She could know what to look for in a relationship, compared with her experience here.

When the bus was loaded Rick took his seat beside Sandy. He took her hand in his and squeezed it, but didn't say anything. They rode in silence for a while, gazing at the grandeur of the landscape. When the castle had receded into the distance, Rick spoke. "This little town we're staying at this evening isn't exactly a nightlife hotspot, but would you like to have dinner tonight? There's this little inn that has the best schnitzel and they even have a live band. How well do you polka?"

"Dinner sounds great, but I'm not sure your feet deserve to polka with me. Would bones broken by being stepped on by one of your tourists constitute a workplace hazard?"

"Don't worry, I'm well insured. And it's hard for you to step on my feet when my feet are busy stepping on yours." He gave her hand another squeeze, then said, "I'm not too worried about that happening. Remember, we did rather well dancing together. We fit perfectly."

"We did, didn't we? I think it must be because we're both bad in the same way, so it just seems right," she said with a halfhearted laugh.

"That may be it," he said, nodding, then he, too, fell silent.

* * *

The bus stopped in front of an ancient inn in a little mountain village whose name Sandy couldn't pronounce. It looked like something out of a picture postcard. After Rick gave Sandy her room key he told her, "You go on up. I'll be by after I take care of some business at the desk and we'll discuss dinner."

Her room upstairs was tiny but cozy, with carved wooden furniture and a diamond-paned window that hung out over the street. She opened the window to find a window box full of red geraniums. The white lace curtains fluttered in the breeze as she went to select a dress for the evening and hang it up so at least some of the wrinkles would fall out of it. She then touched up her makeup and hair, pleased that no traces remained of her tears earlier that day. It wasn't long before there was a knock at the door.

As she expected, it was Rick. She let him in and he shut the door behind himself, then gathered her into his arms and kissed her. She responded eagerly, thrilled with the freedom of acknowledging her feelings at last. It was Rick who eventually broke apart. "This was waiting for you at the desk," he said, handing her an airmail envelope he had been holding in his left hand.

She turned it over and looked at it. There was no return address, and her name was typed above the name and address of the hotel. "Who could have written me here?" she mused.

"The names and addresses of all our hotels were on the itinerary. Did anyone have that?" "

She moved to sit on the end of the bed and he

followed her. "My mother had it, but I don't think she wrote me. She never writes letters."

"Well, open it," he urged, leaning over her shoulder.

She slit the envelope open to find two thin sheets of typewritten letter. As soon as she read the first words, her heart sank and her good mood evaporated.

"Dear Sandy," it said, "We have some unfinished business I feel we need to deal with. Our parting wasn't on the best of terms and I've been doing some thinking."

"Sandy, what's wrong?" Rick's voice cut in.

She glanced up and saw the concern in his eyes. "It's just from someone I really didn't want to hear from."

"You don't have to read it."

But she did. She couldn't help herself. She didn't know what she wanted, whether she was hoping he wanted her back or hoping he gave her yet another reason to hate him. She turned her attention back to the letter.

"I think this was all a mistake from the start," it said. "I'm not sure I ever felt about you the way I should have and I was right to break things off. I wish you could have been reasonable and seen things my way. To be honest, I don't think I ever loved you. You were just someone who was there in the right place and time. Our being together was the result of some bizarre coincidence that we took as the guiding hand of fate.

"I didn't want you to go on being hurt and angry and wanting us to get back together again because there is no chance. I know it seems cowardly for me to write to you when you're so far away, but I feel there is nothing for us to discuss and I wanted to be far enough away you couldn't call. I got the address of a hotel you'd be staying at from your mother. Don't be angry at her, she didn't know what I was going to do."

The letter was signed simply, "Greg." Sandy let the letter fall to her lap and she took a couple of deep breaths to steady herself. She wanted to scream, but Rick's presence stopped her. She tried to fight back the tears that were threatening to fall, but it was futile.

"Sandy?" Rick prodded gently. "What is it?"

Angrily, she thrust the letter into his hands. "Read it," she demanded. "Then you'll understand everything." She got up and went over to the window, gazing outside with unseeing eyes as tears fell unhindered down her cheeks. She heard a muffled curse from behind her, followed by the sound of crumpling paper. Then she felt Rick's hands on her shoulders.

He stood like that for a minute, his strong hands signaling his comforting presence. Finally he said, "Sandy, I'm sorry. I suspected something like that, but I didn't know." His voice was soft and husky. "I shouldn't have pushed you so hard." He seemed to grope for something else to say, but words failed him and he simply repeated, "I'm sorry."

She whirled around and beat at his chest. "I can't believe I wasted so much of my life on him. I dated him for six years. There wasn't anything left to do but get married, and after I'd wasted all that time with him, then he decided he never loved me." Rick didn't flinch from her anger, but just stood there and took it. The knowledge that she was berating an innocent man shook her out of her anger. "I'm sorry, Rick. You didn't deserve that."

He didn't say anything, but instead reached out and brushed the tears off her face. That one gesture shook her composure, and she burst into tears once more. He pulled her to him and let her cry on his shoulder. He held her close, stroking her hair and patting her back. After a minute or two he bent and kissed the top of her head, then her forehead.

"He did you a favor," he murmured after a moment. "I don't know what he's like as a person, but even if he's a wonderful man any girl would want to spend her life with, he did what's best for you."

Sandy pulled away from him quickly. "What gives you that idea?" she demanded angrily, tears still streaming down her face. "You don't even know what happened. You don't know him. You don't know anything!"

Rick just gazed into her eyes, the picture of composure in the face of her anger. "How did you feel about him?" he whispered.

The question shocked Sandy out of her tears. She pulled away from him and said, "What?"

"All that time you were with him, how did you feel?"

She thought for a while, dredging up every memory she could. She tried to recapture the feelings she had when they met, when they first went out, when they first kissed, when he proposed, when he broke off the engagement. It was impossible. She couldn't separate what really had happened from the way her mind had painted the memories. She finally admitted, "I'm not sure."

She knew Gregory had never held her like Rick just had, nor could she imagine crying on his shoulder. He didn't even make her laugh. "He was safe," she whispered. "I was afraid of having to start again with anyone else. It wasn't anything like...like." Sandy suddenly froze with a strange feeling of deja vu. It was happening all over again. She had fallen for the first man she was thrown together with by circumstances. And what did she feel for him but the need to be loved?

"Sandy?" Rick asked, confusion filling his wide blue eyes.

"I'm sorry," she whispered shakily, turning away from him. "I...I think I need to be alone now."

He turned and moved toward the door, then abruptly turned back to face her, his face white, with horror or with anger, she wasn't sure. "You can't keep running," he said with a soft but firm voice. "You have to face life. So what if you made one mistake? Everybody has at least one failed love affair. It happens. You just have to keep trying until you find the right one. Why not take another chance?"

She shook her head angrily. "You don't understand," she whispered, afraid to look him in the eye.

"I think I do. You got involved with one man when you were very young, just because it was convenient and you were afraid to try for anything else. Then you lost him and it hurt. Now you're afraid it's happening again."

"It is!" she shouted. "And it's even worse now. At least with him I got six years of security. There's not even hope for that much with you. You can't even settle down and commit to a life."

He recoiled as if from a physical blow. " 'Maybe not until now," he started, but she cut him off.

"In a few more days we'll say goodbye at the airport and that will be it. I'll go home and you'll find another girl in the next tour group. Maybe it wasn't for real last time, but I've been hurt and I don't intend to hurt like that again."

"Sandy, I'd never hurt you."

"Then leave me alone," she pleaded.

Suddenly angry, he grabbed her by the shoulders. "You are too special a person to allow one mistake to destroy any chance at happiness for you. Sure you may never get hurt again, but will you ever be happy again?" He backed away from her, his eyes blazing. "I love you, believe me when I say that. You've helped me more than you'll ever know. I'll never be the same person again, no matter what happens. All you have to do is trust me and know that I would never do anything I think would hurt you." He turned on his heel and left the room, shutting the door behind him and leaving Sandy feeling more alone than ever.

Rick walked blindly through the inn and out the front door. The evening air was cool, but he didn't notice the chill. He wasn't aware of the distance he had walked until he realized he was out of town on the small hill above the main road. It had been a favorite hiding place for him when he was a young boy visiting the aunt who lived in the town. He had come here instinctively now when he was hurting more than he had ever imagined he could back in those innocent days.

It hadn't been like him to take that kind of a risk in growing to care for someone. It had always been too easy to let his problems solve themselves by simply moving away. He usually only had to wait a year or two at most before his father's next assignment carried him to another home to start anew. Now here was something he couldn't run from, and didn't want to.

If he had only continued his policy of not getting involved with anybody. Then he couldn't have been hurt. But then, he would never have gotten to know Sandy as he had. He would have continued going through the motions in life, never noticing what was around him or seeing the magic in little things. And she probably would never have come out of her shell and reached out to the other people. No, it was worth a little pain on his part.

He also knew he was right that Gregory really had

done what was best for Sandy. Not knowing the man at all, he didn't know if Gregory had let Sandy go out of selfishness or selflessness, but he certainly wouldn't have been doing Sandy any favors by sticking with her in a loveless marriage. Now if only Sandy would realize that and quit letting it hurt her. Rick wished there were something he could do, but that was truly up to Sandy.

He sighed and got up slowly from the rough-hewn wooden bench where he had been resting and headed back to the inn. He came to a stop in front of the inn and stood for a while, staring up at the lighted windows above. Sandy's window was still open, her curtains fluttering in the evening breeze. He wondered if she was still crying or if she'd bothered to go to dinner. He longed to go to her and hold her, to let her cry on his shoulder and get rid of all the pain. His heart almost burst with the longing, but he knew she needed time to heal, and he had to let her grow to trust again. He would only hurt her more if he pressed her now, and he had meant his promise never to hurt her.

He watched her window for several minutes, half hoping she might look out and see him. Then he went up to his own room and struggled through a restless night.

Sandy had cried her heart out after Rick left, then fell asleep, exhausted from the outpouring of emotion. She woke hours later to find that the sun had gone down and that she was hungry. Looking at her watch, she knew she was too late for dinner, but she had some snacks in her tote bag from the last bakery they had passed. She ate several rolls and a couple of rich chocolate bars. She knew it was bad for her, but right now she needed the comfort of bread and chocolate.

After finishing her meager meal she settled down with her computer. She didn't feel like writing, but the end of the tour was approaching and she wanted to at least finish her outline before going back home. When she had left off, the young adventurer had just begun his first attempt to rescue the princess from her enchanted prison. Sandy began writing, taking him ever closer to the fortress, through the secret entrance, and almost to the princess' cell, before he was caught by the wizard and barely escaped with his life. He went off to concoct another plan, based on what he had learned about the wizard's defenses.

Sandy re-read what she had just written and smiled in delight, her pain of earlier in the evening almost forgotten as she lost herself in another world. The story was proving exciting so far, and it was so much fun to write when she could throw in a spell or a potion or two. Just wait until her mother found out what she was writing now! She sighed and leaned back against her headboard. This hero really was wonderful. Imagine a man who risked himself to try to rescue his lady, then when failing once still planned to try again. What she wouldn't give for a hero like that in her life, but, as she reminded herself, there were no knights in shining armor and no princesses held captive behind enchanted walls. There were just men and women struggling to get through life the best they could and dealing with everyday heartache. But wouldn't it be nice if it really were the other way?

Sandy faced the next day with some nervousness. She didn't know how Rick would react to her, or how she would react to him. She felt a stabbing pain in her heart when she saw him at breakfast. He was pale and tired looking, and his eyes were sunken into dark circles. His usual smile was gone, along with the twinkle in his eyes. He acknowledged her entrance with a slight nod, but didn't speak. She gave him a polite smile and took a seat at a different table.

She hurried through breakfast, unable to bear the guilt brought on by his haggard appearance. She was so distracted she didn't even feel a thrill at being able to master her hard roll without concentrating on it. The sound of applause startled her. She turned, half expecting to see a grinning Rick ready to congratulate her on her accomplishment, but it was only Ida and Inez Williamson. Sandy sighed, but she wasn't sure whether she was relieved or disappointed.

"Oh, I'm so glad someone has learned to deal with those horrid things," Ida gushed. "Now teach us how. I'm afraid I'm beginning to waste away from this food. It's just not a proper breakfast." She and her sister pulled up chairs next to Sandy and began serving themselves from the bread basket in the middle of the table.

Despite her glum mood, Sandy had to bite her lip to keep from laughing at the thought of either woman wasting away. They were what could kindly be described as ample. To hide the grin that threatened to break out across her face, she took a hasty sip of coffee. Ida's next comment helped her lose the inclination to smile.

"Now why aren't you with that nice Mr. Hoffman?" Ida asked. "It seemed like you two had really hit it off. You make such a nice couple." She smiled, her eyes starry at perhaps some dimly remembered fantasy of her own.

"Ida, you know that's none of your business!" Inez scolded, and Sandy silently agreed, grateful that she didn't have to come up with an answer. Now that Inez had begun a tirade against her sister, she wouldn't shut up for a while. Sandy hurriedly finished her breakfast, then excused herself and went back to her room to pack.

When she went back downstairs with her luggage, Rick seemed to have regained some of his equilibrium. He wasn't his normal cheery self by any means, but he no longer looked as if his heart was breaking. He checked her off on his list as she boarded the bus, and she took her seat in the old place in the back of the bus near Justin.

The boy greeted her with uncharacteristic enthusiasm when he boarded the bus. "Sandy, that book was great! Thanks!"

She remembered Rick telling her how she had made a difference in this boy's life and her spirits lifted.

"You've finished it already? I'm glad you liked it," she said.

"I liked the part where they were storming the castle," he continued. "That was awesome." His smile faded to a frown. "Are you okay? You look pretty sick."

"I'm not feeling my best," she told him honestly.

"Mr. Hoffman doesn't look too good either. Maybe you two caught the same thing."

"Maybe," she said aloud, while thinking to herself, I know we did.

"I hope you feel better. Say, do you know any other good books like this one?"

She plunged into the welcome diversion whole-heartedly, and the two of them spent much of that morning's drive discussing great adventure books. It was barely noon when they stopped on the shore of a vast lake. Sandy heard Rick's voice coming over the speaker, explaining their location, but she didn't pay much attention. She couldn't hear his voice without remembering the way he had told her he loved her. Instead of listening, she stared out the window. They would be staying at a resort here until the next morning, and she looked forward to the time to rest. The constant travel was beginning to wear her down.

As she unloaded her luggage and carried it into the hotel, she noticed black clouds coming in from over the mountains. Wouldn't you know it, she thought, the one day we're at a resort is the day it decides to rain. The gloomy skies fit her mood perfectly and she decided to spend the afternoon in her room writing. She was lugging her suitcases toward the elevator when she heard a voice call her name. She turned and saw Rick coming toward her. He looked like a man about to have a tooth pulled.

He glanced around awkwardly once she turned toward him. The expression on his face was pained as he said, "Are you going on the tour later on?"

"What tour?" she asked.

"There's a side trip this afternoon to Herrenchiemsee. It's sort of a copy of Versailles on an island in the lake." Suddenly he smiled. "Ludwig built it, so I thought you'd like it."

"Oh," she said as she considered the offer. It would be a group tour, and she didn't want to miss another spectacular castle built by the mad king. Then again, she was afraid that being around Rick much longer would break her resolve, and she'd find herself getting involved with a man only to lose him. While her mind raced, her heart took over and answered for her. "That sounds fun," she heard her own voice saying.

It was as if a light went on inside Rick. His face brightened and his eyes regained their familiar twinkle. "Great. I'll see you at two o'clock," he said, then he turned and walked away toward another group of tourists.

Sandy's own spirits lifted to see him feeling better. It was hurting her to see him so down and to know she was the cause. Maybe he really did care for her. She was beginning to think she loved him. She stifled that thought with another reminder that it was hopeless, and then went up to find her room.

After a quick lunch, Sandy spent her time getting ready for the tour. She selected and discarded half a dozen outfits, finally deciding on a full skirt and a simple blouse, part of her Paris purchases. Flat slippers that would be comfortable for walking completed the outfit. She then spent more than half an hour styling her hair and doing her makeup. When she went downstairs to meet the rest of the group she was feeling good about herself, but she couldn't explain why her appearance had been so important to her.

Rick was looking much more like his usual self. There was some life to his movements, and he had a spring in his step. He acknowledged Sandy's arrival with a smile and a nod, but he didn't interrupt his conversation with the Williamson twins. That irked Sandy a bit. He used to use her as an excuse to avoid them.

When the entire group had assembled they made a short walk to the dock to catch the ferryboat. The sky was growing ever darker, and the wind was picking up, stiffing up waves on the huge lake. Sandy shuddered at the sight and almost turned back, but she was more afraid to admit she was afraid of storms than she was of the storm itself. The thought of braving a storm out on the water was terrifying, but she boarded the boat anyway. She figured that if it were too dangerous they wouldn't let them sail.

The boat ride seemed to last a lifetime to Sandy, rather than the half hour it actually took. The boat didn't toss much in the wind-stirred waters, but Sandy's vivid imagination intensified the tossing. What made her feel even worse was the maddening longing to have Rick near her. To be held in his strong arms would make any of the fear go away. Her lack of self control made her more sick than the motion of the boat on the water did.

What maddened her even more was that Rick wasn't even paying attention to her. He was chatting amiably in German to a couple on the boat. Get it together, Sandy, she told herself. Do you want him to leave you alone or do you want him to pay attention to you? Right now she wasn't sure. Surely the misery of losing him if she allowed herself to get close to him couldn't be worse than the misery of seeing him and forcing herself to keep her distance.

Chapter Nine

Rick noticed Sandy out of the corner of his eye as he chatted with the German couple. She wasn't looking well, and it was his duty to look after her, regardless of any personal feelings either of them might have. He said good-bye to the couple and began trying to make his way over to her. She was very pale and there was a pained expression on her face. Reaching her, he knelt beside the bench where she sat. "Sandy," he said softly, "are you all right?"

She looked up at him and gave him a weak smile that made his heart melt. "I . . . I guess so," she said shakily, then looked away from him. "I'm not a very good sailor when it comes to bad weather." She took a deep, shuddery breath, then looked back at him with a smile that was almost as strong as the one she usually used to challenge him. "Is this the rain you promised?" she asked saucily.

"I'm afraid so. Bad timing, isn't it?" He tried to give her a big grin to match hers. "But don't blame this on me. I didn't promise a storm, just rain."

"I guess you just overdid it this time. Thanks a lot. Did I ever tell you I really don't like storms?"

"No, I don't think it ever came up. So it's your fault. If you had let me know I might have been able to do something about it." She smirked in response, but her face was still pale and drawn. She really did look like she was suffering.

He knelt next to her for a while longer, straining his brain and trying unsuccessfully to think of something casual, yet meaningful, to say. The silence stretched between them, long and uncomfortable. Finally he stood, unable to think of any excuse for remaining next to her. "The ride won't be much longer," he told her. "We're almost there, and then you'll be on solid ground." He turned and walked away reluctantly when she didn't respond to that.

This was harder than he had ever thought it could be. He couldn't bear to be near her without touching her or even speaking to her of anything other than trivial small-talk topics. But if that was what she needed, then so be it. The problem was, she didn't look any happier than he was. He really didn't know what to do. He hoped this castle would cheer her up. It wasn't quite of the fairy-tale splendor of Neuschwanstein, but it was truly glorious.

The boat docked and the group began the walk to the castle. Rick watched Sandy out the corner of his eye, looking for her reaction to the manicured gardens and ornate palace. He longed to see her eyes light up and that smile of wonder spread across her face—

anything but that lost, hurt expression she wore now. The smile would melt his heart, but the sorrow broke it and made it even harder for him to keep from holding her and trying to make the pain go away.

He was disappointed by her reaction, or lack of it, as proved to be the case. He thought he caught a flicker of surprise and delight cross her face, but it was gone before he could be sure. He moved away so that he couldn't see her anymore. Suddenly, he longed for the whole tour to be over with. Surely a clean, cold break would be easier than this daily suffering, and he didn't stand a chance of truly winning her heart if she had closed it to him.

Sandy felt a slight thrill when she saw the massive palace, but she quickly shoved it away. The only way she could keep the pain at bay was to shut out all feelings. If she kept this up she felt she could survive until she got on that plane and went back to her usual life. Then maybe she could allow herself to treasure the memories without feeling the loss quite so much. She didn't know why it should hurt so much to close her heart to a man who said he cared for her, but she knew it hurt more to grow close to someone only to lose him. That was a mistake she would never again repeat, and she could prevent the mistake now by avoiding involvement with a man she knew she would lose soon.

So she built the wall around her heart a little higher and stronger. It was capable of shutting anything out now. To test it, she looked deliberately toward Rick. He was walking rapidly, his hands shoved deep in his jacket pockets. The wind whipped his blond hair across his forehead and he looked as if he were walking against the weight of the world rather than just the wind. Nothing, she thought with satisfaction. No reaction, just a comfortable numbness. She could survive for a while like this. Almost feeling good at her success, she faced the palace and walked on.

As he escorted his group into the front entrance to the palace, Rick noticed the change in Sandy's demeanor. She seemed more at peace and not in so much pain and confusion. Don't flatter yourself, Hoffman, he told himself. She was upset by choppy seas, not by longing for the likes of you. At least it didn't hurt him in quite the same way to see her like that. It was less painful for him to hurt for his own longings than for her pain. As long as she was happy he could be content.

The very thought of that was liberating for a man who had never allowed himself to become close enough to anyone outside his family for him to invest that much of himself in the relationship. Now instead of looking exclusively inside himself, he was turning his concern to someone else. Even if he did lose Sandy, he knew that he would never be the same. He just hoped he wouldn't have to lose her, and he was running out of time.

But he had a job to do, whether or not it was an unwelcome distraction right now. He tried to concentrate on the narrative for the tour of this palace, but he had done it a thousand times and his mind kept straying. He wondered what Sandy's overactive imagination would do with the great hall of mirrors, with its vast windows and thousands of candles that spread light in every direction, reflecting off the gilded mirrors. He was sure she would come up with several suitable stories for the dining table that was raised and lowered so Ludwig could eat alone, and he could just see how the grand staircase would make the ideal setting for a fairy tale. But try as he might, he could see no trace of these imaginings in her face. Her eyes remained cold and her face remained still.

He then threw himself into the guide's spiel with even more enthusiasm, doing everything within his power to pique her interest, but she remained expressionless. He hated to see how someone as captivating as she could be had withdrawn as much as she had. He longed to do something, anything, to bring her back to herself, but he was afraid he might hurt her and he could never do that.

With an inward sigh he continued the tour halfheartedly, anxious to get it over with and get back to his room at the hotel so he could rest and get away from having to see Sandy and be constantly reminded of his pain.

Sandy's carefully built defenses showed dangerous signs of breaking as Rick led them through the magnificent palace. For a moment she imagined him as her hero and herself as the heroine walking arm-in-arm down the great staircase, but she quickly shoved the thought out of her mind. Then when Rick made such an obvious effort to captivate his audience she had almost responded, but again she forced her heart back into its shell. The other tourists were enthralled, and she hoped their response gave him some satisfaction for his efforts.

She was relieved when the tour was finished and they headed back to the dock to catch the boat. While they had been in the palace, the approaching storm had arrived. The wind was whipping furiously and a few drops of rain were falling. She dreaded the short trip back to the hotel on the choppy waters, but she didn't relish being stranded on the island either.

The boat was crowded when they got there, for all the tourists on the island were anxious to get back to shore. Their little group found a corner on an upper deck, where it seemed to Sandy that the rolling motion was worse. She held onto the rail for dear life and squeezed her eyes shut. A touch on her arm startled her, but she didn't have to open her eyes to know who it was. She tried to draw herself further into her fortress, for she was dangerously vulnerable at this moment, what with the pitching of the boat on the storm-tossed lake.

"Are you all right?" came his voice in her ear. She could feel his warm breath on her cheek and she shivered. "Sandy?" he asked again, his voice taut with anxiety when she didn't respond.

She tentatively opened her eyes and immediately wished she hadn't. The water looked black and angry and the waves were capped with white. The sky was as dark as the water, and the horizon seemed to lurch about as the boat tossed. She swayed and squeezed her eyes shut again. A pair of strong arms caught and held her before she could lose her balance. "It's okay, we don't have much longer to go," Rick whispered in her ear. She nodded and clung to him. The stability and comfort of his presence was too important right now for her to worry about whether or not her heart could deal with it.

What surprised her was that he was the one who was shaking. She could feel a slight tremor in the arms that held her, and with her head resting against his chest, she could hear his heart pounding. She didn't think he was afraid of the storm. He didn't seem like he could be afraid of anything—anything, that is, but letting someone get close enough to steal his heart. And he had overcome that fear with her. Then why was he shaking so as he held her?

She wasn't sure if it was an eternity or merely a matter of seconds before the boat became still. "It's all right, we're here," Rick told her. She opened her eyes and looked up at him. From this proximity she could see a strain in his face. He looked tired and hurt, but now that she was close to being on solid ground again she let the barriers come up again and stepped away from him. He dropped his arms from her and let her go without any argument, although she could see the struggle on his face.

As soon as the gangplank was lowered, she hurried off the boat and back to the hotel. A well-timed downpour gave her an excuse to run and not worry about sticking with the rest of the group. Back in her room, she got out of her wet clothes, toweled off and wrapped herself in the plush terrycloth robe that was hanging in the bathroom.

She shut the curtains in the room to shut out the storm and pulled out her laptop computer. Here she was, just a couple of days before she returned home, and all she had done was begin to outline her story. She needed something more to show her mother when she got back. Snuggling into a chair with the computer on her lap, she settled down to come up with a thrilling climax to the tale.

Despite narrowly escaping with his life from his last rescue attempt, the young knight and apprentice magician was making plans to try once more to rescue the princess. He had gathered a group of staunch, though unlikely, allies from among the rebellious outcasts in the nearby town. And, most importantly, he had discovered a spell that could destroy the evil wizard altogether. There was a risk, though. He might not have the strength to use it, and if he did it could take everything he had. But it was a risk he was willing to take so the princess could be freed.

Meanwhile, being the spunky heroine she was, the princess was making her own plans to escape. Sandy's problems were soon lost to her fantasy world as her fingers flew over the computer's keys and she became swept up in her own story.

Several hours later her growling stomach reminded her that if she didn't go down for dinner now she would miss her chance to eat. She quickly pulled on jeans and a sweatshirt and put her hair in a ponytail. Surely most of the rest of the group, including Rick, had already eaten. Grabbing her room key, she hurried down to the dining room.

She was dismayed to find that Rick was just sitting down at an empty table. There was no way she could avoid him without looking rude. She was surprised that he looked a bit uncomfortable when she sat across from him. She would have thought he would have liked that. She forced herself behind her mental barrier and maintained her cool bearing.

While they were waiting for dinner to be brought to them he asked, "How did you enjoy the tour this afternoon?"

She tried to smile, but was afraid the effect must have been ghastly. "It would have been much better if the storm hadn't come up."

He tried again. "What did you think of the castle?"

She honestly could remember little except for the mirrors and some marble. She groped for an answer. "The mirrors were marvelous," she finally said.

His eyes lit up a bit and he seemed to relax with the prospect of some conversation, as trivial as it might be. "That hall of mirrors is one of my favorites too.

You should see it when they light all the candles. The whole room glows.''

She smiled and nodded, and was saved from having to make more conversation by the arrival of the meal. She was famished, so she concentrated on eating. He took a cue from her and ate rather than talking.

When she had eaten all she could, and a little bit more than that, just to avoid conversation, she excused herself and got up from the table. ''I hate to leave you like this,'' she lied, ''but I really have to get some work done. I'll be home in just a couple of days and I want to have something accomplished before I have to go back to the daily grind.''

''I need to be getting back to my room too,'' he told her, rising from the table and walking with her to the lobby. ''I never can seem to get caught up with the paperwork, and I've been neglecting it lately.''

They walked together in uncomfortable silence until they reached her door. ''Well, I guess this is goodnight. Good luck on your work,'' he said, then started to walk away. He turned back as if to add something, but seemed to change his mind and instead went off toward his own room.

Sandy watched him go, then went into her room and picked up her computer to read what she had done that afternoon. Soon she was once again lost in the imaginary world she had created, a place where magic worked, where evil could be conquered with true love and a powerful spell, where the hero of her dreams was always there to come to the rescue, no matter what dangers stood in his path. It was so much easier to retreat into her fantasy world than to deal with the real one, where problems weren't solved with a few well-spoken magical words and a strong sword arm.

Exhausted after several more hours of writing, she reluctantly returned to the real world, leaving her hero on the eve of his fateful assault on the castle. She then shut off her computer and got ready for bed. She fell asleep almost instantly, but didn't get much rest. In her dreams her mind was dealing with all the feelings she had denied during the day. She relived the way Rick had kissed her under the streetlamp, the way he whispered her name, the way he had held her, the look on his face when he had told her he loved her. Her heart ached and she cried silent tears that dampened her pillow.

Rick spent yet another sleepless night. After tossing and turning for hours he finally gave up and sat in the chair by the window, staring into the starless, stormy sky, his thoughts as turbulent as the clouds that boiled above. He was quickly running out of time. Just one more day, then the plane would leave, carrying Cassandra Harrison away from him, possibly forever.

He didn't have high hopes for winning her heart in the few hours he had left. If anything, she seemed even more distant than she had been when he had first met her. At least yesterday she had seemed torn and in pain. Now she seemed content hidden behind those invisible barriers of hers.

He could continue to abide by her wishes and leave her alone, or he could try to force his way through the walls around her heart. Either way, it could be painful for him. If he left her alone his heart might break with the stress, and she might be trapped within those walls forever. That, to him, was the worst possible thing. He had seen how she could be vibrant and passionate, with her quick tongue and active imagination. Now it was painful to see her wrapped up in the shrouds of her past.

But it was a big risk to confront her and force her to trust again. That could hurt them both. He rested his elbows on his knees and buried his face in his hands, groaning with agony. He could never have imagined himself becoming so involved with another person that he could face that kind of dilemma. This was why he had avoided close, long-term relationships for so much of his life. That kind of involvement meant the risk of pain of loss. It was so much easier to keep an emotional distance and start over again repeatedly.

Shaking his head with a sigh, he said to himself, ''When you finally got around to falling in love, why did you have to pick a girl with so much emotional baggage that she's afraid of love?'' But he knew the answer: if he had not been moved by her pain to help her he might never have gone beyond his own emotional walls to reach out to her.

The decision was obvious. He couldn't just let her go. He had one more day, and he would give her that time. But tomorrow night was the deadline. Then he would face her and do everything within his power to convince her to accept him and the love he had to offer. How he would go about doing it, he had no idea, but he was sure his heart would point the way and give him the plan he needed.

Then it struck him. This was too big for him to handle by himself. He needed a few good allies. He was sure he could count on Justin for help. The boy had grown fond of Sandy. Justin's family could be of help as well. Ida and Inez Williamson were such busybodies he knew they would love to get involved, and the elderly Foresters might even take an interest.

Smiling from the heart for the first time in a day, he began to concoct a plan that would be sure to influence Sandy. It wasn't long before sunrise when he finally fell asleep, but this time he was able to rest with an easy heart.

Sandy woke the next morning with a vague memory of disturbing dreams. When she tried to capture the details, they vanished like elusive wisps of smoke. She just knew that for some strange reason she was tired and filled with a sense of loss. She shook off the lingering mood and began steeling herself to face the day.

This was the last day of travel, and as far as she was concerned, this trip couldn't end soon enough. She was sick of living out of suitcases, sick of eating pre-ordered meals in hotel dining rooms, sick of spending hours on the bus and sick of having a certain handsome, blond tour guide wrench her heart every time he smiled at her.

She dressed and packed, but decided against going downstairs for breakfast. She was also sick of hard rolls with marmalade. And, she wasn't quite ready to face Rick yet this morning. The less time she had to spend in his presence, the better. When it was time to load the bus, she collected her bags and went downstairs to the lobby. The rest of the group was gathered there, and Rick was moving through the room with his clipboard, checking off people as they arrived. The bus driver was gathering luggage and carrying it out to the bus. Sandy stiffened as Rick approached her, but he didn't treat her any differently from the other tourists. He gave her a brisk "good morning" and checked her name off his list as the driver collected her suitcase. Then the guide moved on to another tourist.

Sandy was unaccountably miffed at his inattention to her. She was so accustomed to his flattering pursuit of her, and he had been giving her special treatment almost from the moment she had stepped off the plane. Now he was treating her like just another tourist. Although that was what she thought she wanted, it disturbed her. She decided it was just her ego. She liked being flattered, no matter who was doing the flattering.

The more she watched him, the more upset she became. Gone were the longing looks of the day before. Instead, he was downright cheerful, in a better mood than she would have though possible yesterday. She grimaced as he walked past Justin and exchanged high-fives with the boy, then turned and winked at the Williamson sisters, who blushed and tittered. Sandy had a sneaky suspicion that there was something going on she should know about, but she just couldn't put her finger on it.

As soon as the baggage had been loaded, Rick led the group out to the bus. Yesterday's storm had subsided into a steady gray drizzle. The mountains were shrouded in a heavy mist. Sandy settled into her seat on the bus with a sigh. It was just as well that this was the last day of touring. The weather and her mood weren't going to make it a pleasant one.

As soon as he sat down, Justin pulled out a book and began to read. That lifted Sandy's mood a bit, until she heard the familiar beeps and buzzes of the computer game. She turned to see Justin's mother engrossed in the game. Sandy leaned back in her seat with a groan. It looked as if she just couldn't win today. She wanted more than ever to just go home.

A touch on her shoulder shook her out of her thoughts. She turned to see Justin holding little Scott. ''Sandy,'' the boy said. ''My mom's making me hold the little twerp, but I'm trying to read. Could you hold him for a while?''

Sandy gave a resigned sigh and held out her arms for the little boy. He laughed and snuggled into her arms, then began playing with the beads she was wearing. She disengaged the tiny hands, but he grabbed the beads as soon as she let his fingers go. In spite of herself, she found herself laughing with the child, her gloomy mood almost forgotten.

The bus ride into Munich seemed short to Sandy. Scott quickly got bored with the beads and instead snuggled up against Sandy's shoulder, gazing up at her with big, adoring blue eyes. The expression of love freely given melted a hole in the wall around her heart. When the bus stopped near the city center of Munich, she was reluctant to let go of the warm bundle that filled her arms.

Rick led the group through a short walking tour of the old downtown area, but Sandy didn't notice many of the details, just the famous glockenspiel in the city hall tower and the ornate church nearby. She strained her imagination for anything to spark her interest, but her heart wasn't in it.

In contrast, she noticed that Rick was leading the tour with gusto. Instead of giving a dry recitation of names and dates, he was telling stories about the buildings and their former residents that made the history come to life. What truly amazed Sandy was that he wasn't directing his comments to her but rather to the group as a whole. The jealousy she felt bothered her. She should have been relieved.

As the group walked back to the bus, Ida and Inez came up to her and caught her between them. Ida patted her arm warmly and said, "I know just how you feel, dear."

"You do?" Sandy asked, confused about what the question implied.

"Oh, yes. It is hard to believe this is our last day together. It will be so hard to say goodbye to all the new friends we've made and go back home again. Anniston will be so boring after all this."

"Don't be silly, Ida," Inez said. "I'm looking forward to sleeping in my own bed again and not spending the day on the bus."

"Don't be such a spoilsport, Inez," Ida rebutted, showing uncharacteristic pluck with her sister. "Just enjoy the time you're here. I swear, nothing makes you happy. When I find something that makes me happy, I like to hold onto it as long as I can, even if it doesn't last forever, and that's what I intend to do. I'm going to enjoy every last second until the plane lands."

"Hmmph," Inez snorted, but she didn't argue. Sandy felt trapped between the two ladies, but they didn't show any signs of moving on to talk to anyone else. She was grateful to get back to the bus and escape to her seat.

They checked into a hotel near the airport and had lunch, then got back on the bus for a trip to Munich's futuristic Olympic Village. The soaring, airy roof of the stadium was in sharp contrast to the gothic stone of the old city. Rick told of the terror-filled games of 1972, and Sandy got goosebumps, despite her attempts to stay dispassionate. She had to admit he was good at what he did, and deep down inside she felt she had something to do with his restored enthusiasm in his work.

That was a revelation to her. All this time she had focused on what he had done for her, but she had never realized that she had been good for him as well. She was lost in thought, mulling over their mutual needs and how they had met them for each other, when she overheard the Foresters, who were walking behind her.

"Munich sure has changed since the last time I was here," Mr. Forester was saying. "That was back right after the war, not long after we got married."

"I still can't believe we met and got married in less than two weeks that time you were in London just before the war ended. My mother said it was one of those wartime things and it wouldn't last," Mrs. Forester said. Sandy could hear the fondness in her voice.

"Your mother also knew for sure I'd be killed and you'd never see me again," he reminded her.

"I thought it was worth the risk. If I was brave enough to go overseas with the Red Cross, I was brave enough to marry a soldier."

"I'm glad you did," he said.

Sandy blushed as she overheard such a private conversation. Then the Foresters passed by her. "Have you enjoyed your trip, dear?" Mrs. Forester asked Sandy as they passed. The old couple slipped their arms around each other, chuckling at some private joke. Sandy sighed and followed them back to the bus.

All too soon, it was over. When they headed back to the hotel for the evening, the trip was almost concluded. All that was left was the night, then they took off from Munich's airport the next morning. Tomorrow night Sandy would be sleeping in her own bed back in Dallas. She wasn't sure how she felt about that. In a way she felt there was so much more to see and do in Europe, but at the same time she knew she would be much more comfortable away from the disturbingly handsome and charming tour guide.

She glanced at Rick as she waited for the elevator to take her up to her room, but he didn't look back at her. She had a dreadful sense of finality. She didn't know what she expected or wanted him to do, but it bothered her that he had just given up. She had a sudden longing to go to him, to beg him to spend those last few hours with her, but she didn't dare. That would be foolish and impractical, and she had never done a foolish, impractical thing in her life. She reminded herself that by this time tomorrow she would be in an airplane over the Atlantic, separated from Rick by an ocean. Now was no time to get anything started.

Rick knew his time was running out. It didn't look as if Sandy would turn around of her own accord, despite the efforts of his allies. She seemed even more distant than yesterday. He looked for her at dinner, hoping to at least sit at the same table with her, but she didn't show up. At least that gave him the excuse he needed to go to her room and talk to her. He just hoped the Foresters and the Williamsons had managed to plant a few seeds for thought in her brain.

When the meal was over with, he went back to his

own room to get his thoughts together. He also primped a bit, making sure his hair was in place and his shirt was unwrinkled. Then he took a few deep, calming breaths, thought of and discarded a dozen opening lines, then made his way to Sandy's room. Steeling his resolve, he knocked briskly at her door. He heard some shuffling on the other side, then Sandy's voice said, "Who is it?"

"It's Rick. I noticed you weren't at dinner, so I thought I'd check on you. There were also some last-minute announcements you missed." He was very glad he'd thought of that last part during dinner; it made his excuse seem less feeble.

There was a scraping on the other side of the door as she disengaged the chain and fumbled with the lock. She opened the door slightly and peeked through the crack. Her hair was disheveled and her face was pale. "I'm sorry I missed the last dinner," she murmured. "I wasn't feeling well."

"I'm sorry to hear that. May I come in? I'd rather not disturb your neighbors by talking in the hall."

"Oh, yes, of course." she opened the door fully and stepped back so he could enter. As he shut the door behind himself she scurried over to the far side of the room and sat in the chair beside the bed, putting the bed between them. She crossed her arms over her chest and asked, "What was it I missed?"

He cleared his throat, trying to fight back the nervous tension, then started telling her about departure and customs procedures. "We'll be leaving the hotel at nine tomorrow morning. Your flight is at noon. To make customs easier, I suggest you make a list of purchases you made while abroad and their prices."

Chapter Ten

Sandy felt her heart sink when Rick launched into his boring discourse on customs procedures. She didn't know what she expected—maybe a desperate, heartfelt declaration of love? She certainly hadn't given him any reason to think she'd be the least bit receptive to such a thing, but it was still a blow to her ego to have him give up on his pursuit of her so easily. She mentally kicked herself for having any such thoughts at this late stage.

He finished his little speech and asked, "Was that all clear? Do you have any questions?"

"Oh, it's all clear," she said, although she hadn't heard a word.

He nodded. "Fine. Fine. That's great." He turned as if to go, and Sandy's heart leapt when he turned back to her. "If you think of any questions, let me know," he said. Sandy could cheerfully have smashed his face in, or else jumped into his arms and kissed him so warmly he wouldn't want to leave. Instead, she did nothing but watch him turn back toward the door.

He opened the door, then paused with his hand on the doorknob. After a moment in which the tension in the air around him was almost tangible, he abruptly shut the door and whirled to face her.

"I just can't do it," he said, half to himself. "I know it's what you want, but I don't think it's what's good for you, or for me, for that matter. I can't let you just go off on your own, still afraid of trusting or loving another person." She was too stunned to respond. Here he was saying what she had hardly dared hope deep in her heart, but she didn't know what to do. So, she just listened.

"It's not me you're afraid of, or anyone else. It's you," he said as he paced nervously back and forth across the room, avoiding eye contact with her. "You're afraid of yourself, of letting go and trusting yourself to remain whole while giving yourself to another person. If I let you go now you'll just keep on that way, and I love you too much to see that happen to you," he told her, his eyes flashing stormy blue. She was reminded of the night in the vineyards over the Moselle River, but now his voice wasn't soft and gentle. It was firm and ringing with conviction.

Finally, she found her tongue. "What do you want?" she whispered.

He paused in his anxious pacing and looked her in the eye. "What do you mean?"

"I mean this is the last night we'll be together. Tomorrow I'm going back home. That's in another country, on another continent. That doesn't leave us

much time for forging bonds of trust or anything like
that.''

He threw up his arms in exasperation. ''I'm talking
about something permanent, forever, sharing lives.''

''Forever?!'' she gasped. This was too much. It was
as if he had read every mental script her mind had ever
created for this sort of encounter. She felt herself falling
dizzily, although she was firmly planted in her chair.

''Yes, forever,'' he said with conviction. ''Are you
afraid of that?'' He didn't wait for an answer, but sat
on the corner of the bed and gestured helplessly with
his hands. ''I don't know about all those things they
say you should look for in someone you marry, and I
know ten days isn't exactly a long courtship. But what
I do know is that when we're not letting our past hang-
ups get in the way, we bring out the best in each other.
I think that says a lot, and I wonder how much I could
grow in a lifetime with you if you've given me so much
in such a short time.''

Sandy was overwhelmed. She hadn't been expecting
him to have such logical, well-articulated arguments.
He was making sense, and her head was reeling. Her
heart wanted to accept and believe everything he said
while her mind was reminding her that she wanted to
avoid getting close to anyone. While her thoughts
churned, her mouth responded as if it were the most
logical thing to do. ''That's fine,'' she said. ''But you
seem to be forgetting that I leave tomorrow. That's all
the forever we've got.''

''Says who?'' he shouted defiantly. ''I told you I

wanted to move back to the States to start marketing my tours. Dallas would make a great base of operations for me. I could be there in a few months and we could pick up where we left off.''

She shook her head. "No good. That sounds like a line, and I've heard a few too many good lines from men. You're especially good at them. How do I know I'll ever see you again once I get on that airplane? I'm sorry, but I don't think I could deal with another broken heart just now."

He gazed earnestly into her eyes, and she could feel the force of his love burning to her soul. Her knees went watery and she had to restrain herself from throwing herself into his arms and begging him to hold her forever. But her mind won out and she remained in her chair, locked in mesmerizing eye contact with him.

"You just have to trust me," he whispered, then frowned. "No, I can't ask you to do that. You aren't ready." Suddenly he flung himself across the bed, grabbed the phone on her nightstand and began dialing. When he got an answer on the other end of the line he started speaking in German, but after glancing at Sandy he switched to English.

"Erich," he said, "Are there any seats left on that plane out of Munich tomorrow? The one the group's booked on?" He paused and listened to the response, then went on. "Great. I want you to book me on that flight, if you can." He held the receiver away from his ear and Sandy caught the sounds of irate German streaming from its speaker. "Yes, you did hear right. I want on that flight," Rick insisted.

He listened to more protests, then when it appeared he had gotten his way he continued. "Now, are seats all assigned yet? I want you to put me next to a Cassandra Harrison. Yes, I know that's in first class. Just reserve the ticket, all right? And could you send the rest of my luggage down to Munich on overnight express? Thanks, Erich. Yes, I will come back from time to time, I'm just going to start the stateside part of our operation a little sooner. Yes, now. I'll explain later."

He hung up and looked directly at Sandy. "Now do you believe me?"

"I believe you're crazy." She shook her head in astonishment. "To just throw everything together and jump on a plane at a moment's notice, that's insane."

"It's not as though I had to throw everything together. I never unpack."

"That's just it!" she shouted, tears beginning to stream down her face. "You never settle down, you never unpack, you never commit. Me? I like stability and peace and quiet. I like my ordinary, uneventful life. I prefer to write my adventures instead of living them."

"Is that the case?" he said softly. "Or do you like buying fancy green silk dresses in Paris boutiques, dancing 'til dawn at seedy dives, challenging small children to video game tournaments and imagining yourself a princess in every castle? You don't have to hide from yourself."

She couldn't look in his eyes anymore without falling hopelessly in over her head. She turned away and bit her lip, trying to fight back the tears that were spilling from her eyes. "I just don't know what to think," she whispered, as much to herself as to him. "I'm not even sure I'm ready for something like this."

"If you need to think, I'll give you all the time in the world. But I'm going to be on that plane tomorrow. I won't let you go, believe me."

She turned to look at him, and that was her undoing. With a strangled sob, she reached for him and fell into his arms. He held her close, as if he were making good on his promise to never let her go right then.

Then her mind took over and brought her back to reality with a resounding crash. She still wasn't sure she was ready for this. Suddenly, she pushed herself away from him. "I—I have to think. Please," she stammered.

He took a step away from her. "You're right. Please do think. I want you to be as sure of this as I am. I'll see you in the morning." Before she could say anything else, he had left the room.

She collapsed onto the bed, her head reeling with conflicting emotions. He had been able to make her laugh when nothing else could. He made her feel good about herself, and in feeling good about herself she had learned to reach out and touch others. He was right. He had brought out the best in her. He had encouraged parts of her character she hoped she never lost. But this was a big step. It frightened her that a man would be willing to follow her to another continent. Sandy Harrison wasn't the kind of woman who inspired that kind of devotion.

No, but Cassandra Harrison might. Rick had taught her that, that she shouldn't sell herself short by hiding away behind preconceived ideas about herself. Sandy Harrison wasn't the kind of woman to promise to marry a man she had known ten days, either. Was Cassandra? That was what she had to determine. Still pondering the decision, she got ready for bed, even though she knew it was hopeless. There was no way she would get much sleep that night.

She did sleep some, although not well, and she woke still not knowing what to do. She went through the motions of packing, her thoughts more on the decision she had to make than on her work. Even though he had announced his intentions of going back to the States with her no matter what she decided, she felt it was only fair to him to tell him before the plane left whether or not she would accept him. She didn't want him to disrupt his life over her for nothing.

She also found herself pondering the things she had heard the Williamsons and Foresters say the day before. She could hardly imagine the Foresters meeting and marrying within just a couple of weeks. In that situation, she wasn't sure she could have taken the risk to marry someone she might never see again. Yet it was hard to imagine a happier couple. Their marriage had stood the test of time.

And what was it Ida had said about holding onto the things that made her happy? Sandy shook her head and tried to concentrate on her packing, suddenly aware that today she would have to say goodbye to everybody from the trip. What she had to decide was whether she would be saying goodbye to Rick as well.

He didn't speak to her when she saw him at breakfast. He just caught her eye in a gaze that made her knees weak. She knew him well enough to know he wouldn't press her. He would just wait for her decision, but she didn't know what to tell him yet.

All through the process of checking out of the hotel and loading the bus her thoughts continued to spin in circles. She managed to mumble a few replies to Justin's excited narration of his favorite parts of the trip, but her mind was elsewhere. Finally she decided that this wasn't a decision that could be made through clear, cold logic. There were so many pros and cons that she wasn't sure where the balance lay. She would have to decide with her heart, and that meant trusting both herself and him.

They unloaded at the airport, and their luggage was whisked away by baggage handlers. Sandy was so lost in thought that she didn't notice that Rick wasn't with the group anymore until she looked for him, hoping that perhaps the sight of him might help her make her decision. When she had convinced herself that he really wasn't there she felt a rising tide of panic.

She had let him get away, she knew. She had dithered long enough over the decision that he had given up. She didn't think that was really like him, but she couldn't blame him for not wanting to get hurt.

Suddenly, as soon as she felt the fear of losing him, she knew what her decision was. She didn't want to have this feeling of having lost him again. It wasn't that she wasn't complete without him; she just was more complete with him. Now in his absence she felt the loss. Now if only she hadn't really lost him for good.

Forcing herself to calm down, she remembered all he had said about trust. Now that she had trusted herself enough to commit to him, she had to trust him. There surely must be some business he had to take care of before they left, she reasoned. There was still an hour before the flight left.

Too anxious to sit, she put her carry-on luggage into a pile by the gate and paced the waiting area, trying not to crane her neck to watch all the approaches to the area. As she paced, she analyzed and reanalyzed her decision, but now that she had made it she knew there was no going back. She wanted to be with him. She was happier with him than without him and she loved him and knew he loved her enough to put his heart on the line. She glanced at her watch and then back and forth down the concourse. He still had half an hour to make it.

To distract herself, she tried to think of her story. She was so close to finishing her outline, but she wasn't sure exactly what would happen next. She did know that the hero would defeat the wizard and escape with the princess to live happily ever after, but she didn't know how to get there from where she was. She thought back over the plot and characters that she had, and then it dawned on her.

She had been writing about her own situation all along. Here she had been dreaming of the brave magician/knight who risked his life to save his princess, and who braved even greater danger to keep trying despite his failure. There had been no need to dream, for this was what she had all along. Scaling the walls around her heart had surely been as difficult as any enchanted castle, and he had risked that for her.

The plane that would carry her home had connected to the jetway and the flight crew had boarded, and still there was no sign of Rick. Sandy was fighting to restrain the tears that wanted to burst from her when she heard her full name gasped breathlessly from behind her. She turned and saw Rick, standing with a huge bouquet of red roses in his arms. He was panting and flushed.

He handed her the roses, then dropped to one knee and fumbled in his jacket pocket. "I realized I'd been remiss," he told her. "Imagine, proposing to a lady without being the least bit prepared. No flowers, no ring, nothing. And proposing like that to a certified hopeless romantic! You're probably an expert on how it's done, and I really messed up." He pulled a small velvet box from his pocket, opened it and took out a glittering ring. Then he took her hand in his and asked sincerely, "Cassandra Harrison. I love you and want to spend the rest of my life with you. Will you marry me?''

Fighting to restrain the laughter and tears that threatened to overwhelm her at this wonderful, hilarious gesture, she said simply, ''Yes.''

He gaped at her. ''Yes?''

''Yes,'' she confirmed. ''Now put the ring on my finger and get up. People are beginning to stare.''

''What? Oh, yeah.'' He slipped the ring on her finger then stood up. ''Let them stare,'' he said huskily as he pulled her to him and kissed her soundly. Sandy shrieked as the thorns in the roses she still held were pressed against her chest by his sudden embrace. ''Sorry,'' he said sheepishly, stepping away from her.

She couldn't contain her laughter anymore. ''Oh, Richard Hoffman, you crazy, wonderful amazing man. This is truly the most incredible proposal I've ever heard of. I don't think I could have come up with something like this even in a book.'' She dropped the roses on a chair, then pulled him back towards her and kissed him.

By this time all the passengers had gathered around the spectacle, and they applauded when the couple kissed. They broke off, embarrassed, and Sandy asked him softly, ''I take it you vanished to find the flowers and the ring?''

''Right. I didn't think it would take long at all, but I forgot that the jewelry store is at the other end of the airport and then I had to try two florists to find the right flowers.''

"You really had me worried there. I thought you'd given up on me."

"Didn't I tell you I never would?"

"Yes, and I had to trust myself to trust you. That was when I knew I wanted you."

"Oh, so it wasn't the flowers."

She smiled. "No, it wasn't the flowers. It was you. I just want you to promise one thing."

"What's that?"

"That you'll never stop making me laugh. We're off to a good start now."

He smiled back at her. "I promise. Though I don't know if I can live up to the humor level of that proposal." They both laughed at that, and he added, "I guess we'll have something interesting to tell our kids. 'Daddy proposed by dropping to one knee in the middle of an airport and apologizing for not doing things right the night before after running all over the place looking for a ring and some flowers.'"

Their flight was announced and as the passengers began boarding, Rick picked up Sandy's carry-on bags. "Did you check your luggage?" she asked him.

"I told you, I was getting on this plane no matter what."

"Yes, you did. I still can't believe you're doing something this crazy. And you called me the hopeless romantic."

"Well, maybe you can use this in one of your books."

She gave him a mysterious grin. ''Maybe I already have.''

He looked at her in surprise, but she just smiled at him as she thought of the dashing hero of her book who risked life and limb to snatch his true love from the jaws of a fate worse than death. So maybe she really hadn't been in peril and he hadn't risked his life, but it was close enough for her.

She remembered his remark that maybe those mythical characters still existed, but in a modern guise. She wondered for a moment if a windbreaker was the modern equivalent of shining armor, then sneaked another glance at him and smiled. Yes, he had been right.